SOULS FOR SALE

Asta Idonea

When demon Saul persuades comic book artist Tom to sign over his soul in exchange for a night of passion, little does he know what lies in store. Demons can't fall in love—or so he's been told—but he finds himself smitten and attempts to destroy the contract, desperate to save Tom from an eternity of torture.

With Saul and Tom forced to run, a showdown between Heaven and Hell ensues as the angels and demons argue over who owns Tom's soul. But does either party have a stronger claim than Saul?

A NineStar Press Publication

Published by NineStar Press
P.O. Box 91792,
Albuquerque, New Mexico, 87199 USA.
www.ninestarpress.com

Souls for Sale

Printed in the USA
First Edition
March, 2018

Print ISBN: 978-1-948608-30-5

Also available in eBook, ISBN: 978-1-948608-26-8

Warning: This book contains sexually explicit content, which may only be suitable for mature readers.

Prologue

SAUL

It's tough being a demon in this day and age. Times are hard and souls just aren't what they used to be. I should know; it's my job to collect them. Or try to, anyway. What I wouldn't give to go back to the good ol' days when you could buy a soul as easily as an apple at the marketplace. And I mean a proper apple, plucked straight from the tree that morning. None of this modified, refrigerated crap that passes as fresh fruit nowadays.

I know what you're thinking. Trust me; I've heard it all before. You're wondering how it could be so hard to get someone to sign away their soul in an age when everything can be obtained for a price, when everything is for sale. Actors, bankers, politicians. You'd think rich pickings; am I right? Well, you'd be wrong.

Problem is that no one believes anymore. Picture this: I walk up to someone and offer to grant them anything their heart desires in exchange for their soul. Now, in times past they'd either tremble in fear and drop to their knees, praying to the guy upstairs (my cue to leave), or they'd tremble in fear for a moment and then sign on the dotted line. Simple. Everyone knew where they stood. But if I were to try that today, most people would laugh in my face and walk off, or else they'd look uneasy and slink away from the 'deranged lunatic' as soon as possible. Hell, I miss the fear.

The faith is gone, you see, supplanted with technology, gizmos, and gadgets. An age of information. Everything you want, obtainable at the press of a button. What is there to long for anymore? What is there worth selling your soul for that you couldn't get another way? Sure, you still have the old standards, the favourites—riches, power, and sex—but as I said, the belief is sadly lacking.

Every passing year it gets harder and harder to fill my quota. I have the boss breathing fire down my neck—both metaphorically *and* literally—and damned if I know how to get around the problem. It's not just me. My colleagues are equally exasperated. It won't be too much longer until it's impossible to sign up even one new soul to burn in everlasting Hell. Then what's a conscientious, hard-working demon to do?

Anyhow, I guess it's about time I introduced myself. The name's Saul. Yeah, I know, but it's not like I picked it. We get what the boss dishes out, and I drew the short straw that day. Guess he was in one of his funny moods. I'm here today following a mark. I'm actually pretty stoked I found this guy, as he's shaping up to be the most promising potential soul-seller I've seen in several months. Hey, try saying *that* three times fast! The trick now is not to rush things, not to push him too hard or too fast.

Oh, here he comes. See if you can pick him from the crowd. No? Hard, isn't it? Everyone looks the same these days. It used to be so much easier to tell a sinner from a saint. Now the line is so blurred it barely exists at all.

But I digress. Just wait a moment... There! See the guy heading into the pub? The one in the Marvel T-shirt? With the blond curls? That's our man. Bit of a stereotype of a comic-book nerd, isn't he? Unlikely to sell his soul, you think? Well, we'll soon see.

Chapter One

SAUL

I enter the pub, saunter to the bar, and settle on one of the stools. This isn't the most salubrious joint on the block and the stool wobbles precariously on uneven legs under my weight. I grip the counter for a moment, until equilibrium returns, and then assess the situation. So long as I don't make any sudden moves, I should be safe. The last thing I want is to fall on my arse. Not the kind of first impression I'm hoping to make on my mark.

The barman waddles over and raises an expectant eyebrow. He scans my attire. From the twist of his lips, I deduce that he agrees with my own belief: I look wildly out of place here. Nonetheless, I don't suppose he's going to toss me out. Money is money whether it comes from a lint-lined pocket in a pair of faded, torn jeans or from a genuine leather wallet, produced from the inner pocket of a bespoke suit jacket.

I had planned to plump for a reliable half-pint of *Old Peculiar*, but then the guest ales catch my eye. "A pint of the *Green Daemon*, thanks," I say as I place a tenner on the sticky bar top.

What can I say? I have a sense of humour—sue me. Besides, I love the little devil figure grinning out at me from the label. And, hey, I *am* wearing a green shirt and beautifully coordinated tie today. It must be serendipity.

The barman sets the beer in front of me and drops a handful of change beside it. I scoop up the coins and thrust them into my pocket. Then I lift the glass to take my first sip. It's not bad; there's a fruity aroma. I'd probably pair it with an Asian fusion dish, if that sort of thing interests you. But I'm not here to entertain or offer culinary advice. I have work to do.

The mirror behind the bar gives me an excellent, if somewhat smeary, view of the room, and it doesn't take me long to spot my mark again. He's in the corner seat—the darkest spot in the pub—and is nursing a half-pint of something that looks suspiciously like a girly cider. Geez, the guy is staring into the glass like it's a fricking crystal ball. What is it he expects to see in there—a masterpiece by Dalí?

Hey, I'm not mocking the guy. He's actually pretty cute in all his dorkish glory. If you're into that sort of vibe. One look at him, sitting there like a dejected puppy, is enough to convince me I'm on the right track. I can even guess his wish. Oh yes. Numero tres for this dude. Sex, sex, sex. The poor sap looks like he hasn't been laid in a lifetime, if ever, and as a fellow man—or close enough—it's my duty to help him out. If he happens to sign a little contract in the process, all the better...for me, anyway.

I've decided on my play, but I watch the guy for a few more minutes, choosing the best approach. The trick to a successful signing is to make the initial contact count. I should probably have an honorary psychology degree since the most important part of this job is reading your mark. You have to know what they want, but more than that, you have to know *how* they want it. You've got to understand how people tick. Know what I'm saying?

Take this guy. We can see he desires sex, but what does he like? Is he into blondes or brunettes, curves or willows? These are all vital questions because I need to know how to alter my appearance before I go over to him. Yeah, you heard me right. The things I do for this job! Believe me, temporary loss of my favourite anatomical parts is the *least* of it.

Once again, it makes one long for the good times past. Back then it was a simple matter of two choices. First, male or female, depending upon my target, and second, handsome or deformed. Most wanted the devil to be handsome. I guess it was easier to sin if you looked upon a pretty face while you were about it. However, there were always a few who wanted to be truly horrified by what they were doing, to feel the weight of it. In those cases, the traditional horns, cloven hooves, and tail were my attributes of choice.

Nowadays, people are so picky. So many choices, so many new and convoluted kinks to work into the equation. This guy doesn't seem to be the kinky type on the surface, but you never can tell. Does he want the sweet girl next door? Does he want a dominatrix, all whips and leather? Does he want...a man?

I temporarily lose my train of thought, and my jaw drops quite of its own accord.

Even as I jabber away, I have been keeping half an eye on my mark. He completely ignores the young waitress attending the couple two tables down from him, but his gaze *is* captured by a waiter who's just exited the kitchen. The man is lean but toned, and he flicks his head to shift choppy brown locks out of his eyes as he adjusts his grip on the plates he carries hurriedly across the room.

I confess I didn't see that coming. Not on this occasion.

My guy's practically salivating as he follows the man with his gaze. Given the flush in his cheeks, I wouldn't be the least surprised if he had a hard-on; although, it's impossible to verify that with the table in the way.

One thing is clear: this wasn't a chance encounter. No, he's been waiting to catch a glimpse of this guy. Suddenly, I understand his reason for choosing this completely hideous pub. No. Scratch that. They do have a pretty good list of guest ales. Let's call it a semi-hideous pub, in the interest of fairness.

The waiter-god, his work completed, strolls back into the kitchen, leaving the door swinging to and fro in his wake. My guy watches it like a hawk long after it ceases to move, no doubt hoping for a repeat performance. When the door stays resolutely closed, he shifts his attention back to his untouched drink.

Well.

I confess that the revelation threw me for a moment. Even a seasoned professional such as myself can occasionally be caught off guard. No one's perfect, after all. But I'm nothing if not adaptable, and it doesn't take me long to bounce back and rethink my plan of attack.

I'll be able to keep my man-parts for this one—always a blessing—but one thing still needs to be decided: how should I appear to him? The obvious option is to turn myself into the waiter. I'm guaranteed a good reception that way, and yet I'm tempted to try something different and approach him in my own form.

Now, I don't like to brag, but I consider myself to be quite the looker. Well, you're looking at me now. Wouldn't you agree? And I'm actually not too dissimilar from the object of our guy's affections. Sure, my hair's darker, closer to black, but I have a toned, compact figure like him and commensurate sharply defined cheekbones. Why not give it a try? I can always make a second approach as the waiter if this one goes pear-shaped.

My mind made up, I hop down from the bar stool and amble towards the gents. I move nice and slow, with a good sway of the hips that stays on the right side of being camp. I want to make sure he gets a good look at me as I pass, and judging by the weight of the gaze I feel upon me, I've succeeded. Time for step two.

Chapter Two

TOM

I don't know what I'm doing here. Well, I do, but I'm trying not to admit it to myself. I can't pretend that I'm here to meet someone—who would I have to meet? This isn't the sort of place you frequent for the amazing ambience, nor the sublime cuisine. Really, I don't even want this drink that sits before me; I only bought it because you can't go into a pub and sit for an hour without ordering something. Do I like cider? I can't recall ever trying it, but it's my go-to beverage here, the first thing that pops into my head when asked what I want. Ordering a Coke seems too juvenile. Not that it matters, I suppose. To date, I've left every drink untouched and I feel no enthusiasm to go against that precedent today.

A door hinge squeaks to my left. I look around. And there he is, at last. He doesn't look at me—not so much as a glance. Why would he? Nevertheless, I follow him with my gaze as he carries two steaming plates to a table across the room. Job done, he turns and strides back towards me.

Part of me begs him not to suddenly notice me and catch me staring. The other part longs for him to meet my eye and smile. Of course, in my daydreams, he does that and more. In fantasies, he captures my gaze, approaches, sits beside me, takes my hand, leans in, his lips brush mine, and… Well, you get the idea. The reality is that I don't even know his name. I do know that he's straight. He only flirts with the few female customers, and I once caught sight of him embracing the waitress before the kitchen door swung closed. It's utterly hopeless; I realise that. Yet I can't seem to let go.

I first encountered Mr Tall-Dark-And-Handsome a few weeks ago. I was walking by and spotted him delivering meals to a table by the window. God, but he looked gorgeous. The next day, I found myself taking the same route. The day after that, I ventured inside, and over the past few weeks it's become my lunchtime routine. Not once has he so much as registered my presence. That's nothing new—most people don't. However, just seeing him brightens my day.

I fear my actions border on stalking, but I aim to stay on the right side of that invisible line. Nothing can come of this. I have no designs. There is no 'us' in the future. Nonetheless, here I sit, day after day, basking in a few precious seconds of his presence.

The truth is I'm lonely. How do all those couples out there do it? How do they find one another and form relationships? I mean, I've had partners before—I'm not that sad virgin mainstream media make out all nerds to be—but nothing meaningful, nothing lasting. Is there someone out there for me? How will I ever find Mr Right when I seem to be invisible to the population at large?

I'm pondering this life dilemma when another patron captures my attention. He was seated at the bar with his back to me, and I'd not given him more than a passing glance, but now he stands and heads towards the toilets, affording me an opportunity to see him better.

He's handsome. That's my first impression. A subtle sway to his hips lets me appreciate his slim, toned frame. He reminds me of the waiter in a vague, external way. They're both tall and dark. Yet, there's something more to this guy—an aura—that makes him stand out. He doesn't look directly at me; however, as impossible and unlikely as it seems, I get the sense that he knows I'm there and a shiver runs down my spine.

When he enters the gents and the door swings shut behind him, I release a breath.

What am I doing? First the waiter, now this stranger. I should get up, walk out, and never return. However, my body makes no attempt to follow through on this fine suggestion. I tell myself that my mind is made up. This fascination with random men whom I can never have is at an end; I'm turning over a new leaf. My legs choose not to believe me. Either that or they're simply ignoring me and forming a splinter party within the democratic body of Thomas Ives.

I glance at my watch. It's too early to go home. Neither do I feel inclined to head back to the office. I finished ten panels this morning, so it's not as if I have any urgent work to complete; I'm well ahead of schedule already. Another twenty minutes here won't hurt. Maybe thirty. After that, I'll definitely leave.

Chapter Three

SAUL

I spend a couple of minutes in the gents just waiting, entertaining myself by reading the graffiti (mostly misspelled) and avoiding the many dubious wet patches on the floor, some of which I don't even want to contemplate. Normally, I'd drag my stay out a little longer, but my nostrils can't bear any more, so at the count of one hundred I remove my jacket, drape it over my arm, and head back out to the bar.

I pretend to trip over the leg of a chair as I pass my mark's table. Clichéd, I know, but sometimes the classics are the best. I shoot out a hand to steady myself and the table wobbles, spilling his drink. (The glass is still so full I don't even need to go for an all-out knock-over move.)

"Aw, geez. I'm sorry, friend." I right myself and offer an apologetic smile, running a hand through my hair at the same time to give him a flash of my biceps.

"It's fine. Really." He looks a little like a deer caught in the headlights. It's actually pretty cute.

"Let me buy you another. No, I insist," I add when he opens his mouth to protest.

I mark my territory by leaving my jacket on the seat beside him. Then I wander to the bar and place the order.

"Mind if I join you?" I ask when I return with our beverages. "It's so dull to drink alone, don't you think?"

He's still looking startled, but I take the lack of resistance as an affirmation, and after setting the drinks on the table, I wriggle into the seat next to him, taking the place of my jacket, which I move onto my lap. I push his drink across the short space between us. "The name's Saul."

"Thomas. Thomas Ives."

"And do people call you Tommy?"

"No. Tom. Sometimes."

From the tone he uses, I interpret 'sometimes' as 'never'. It seems a good opportunity to remedy that, not least because it offers me an in.

"Well, a pleasure to meet you…Tom." I roll the name gently off my tongue so it sounds like a purr. Let him imagine hearing me say it in bed. To give him a moment for this reflection, I take a sip of my drink. The action makes him reach for his, too, although all he does is nurse it between his hands. I nod towards his T-shirt. "Cap or Iron Man?"

"I'm sorry?"

"Who'd win the fight? Cap or Iron Man?" (Another trick for soul-scamming in the modern age: know your pop culture.)

He ponders this for a moment. Obviously it's a deeper and more poignant question than I'd thought. I'll have to remember that for the future. Perhaps I'll bring it up again at some classy literary event and see what reaction it gets.

"Iron Man," he decides at last. "It'd be close, but Iron Man has the better weaponry."

"I'd plump for the Cap myself, but then I've always been partial to a blond."

I punctuate this statement by giving him a quick look up and down. He gulps and lowers his gaze to his glass. An attractive blush mottles his cheeks.

It's a bold move so early in the conversation. I couldn't have made my interest more obvious if I'd held a flashing neon sign above my head. But I find I'm starting to enjoy myself. He's a bit of a nerd, but Tom has looks, and I'm as partial to a pretty face as any man. Given my nature, I'm pretty fluid. Girls or guys. I'll swing either way—and anywhere in between.

My plan had been to seduce him as myself—get his juices flowing and all that jazz—and then offer him the waiter to sweeten (and hopefully seal) the deal. Now, I'm experiencing a change of heart. Why not set myself a little challenge and make myself the main reward?

Yep, if he signs on the dotted line, he gets one night of unbridled passion with yours truly. Not to blow my own trumpet or anything, but it'd be a much better deal for him. I'm fairly certain the waiter's straight, for one thing. I wouldn't be surprised if he's feeling up that waitress out back even as we speak. For another... Well, let's just say, no one—male or female—has ever finished a night with me feeling in any way...unsatisfied. If you get my meaning. I've got the moves, baby. Austin Powers, Don Juan, Casanova. They have nothing on me.

"So, what is it you do, Tom?" Time to get the conversation moving again.

He starts. "Do?"

"You know, for work, employment."

"Oh." He visibly relaxes. "I do artwork. On comic books and graphic novels."

Figures. "Must be fun. Get to set your own hours a bit?"

He nods. "As long as I meet my deadlines, I can go into the office whatever time I please."

"Sweet. Nothing like beating the nine-to-five daily grind. What I wouldn't give for such a life. With me, it's nose to the grindstone day in and day out. One toe out of line and the boss hails down fire and brimstone. And trust me when I say that you don't want to be on the receiving end of that!"

His eyebrows arch. "Damn. Sounds rough. What is it you do?"

Finally, Tom is engaging and things are looking up. (Hopefully in more ways than one.) "Oh, I guess you could say I'm in procurement. Of a very particular kind."

"Ah."

Nothing more to add, comic boy? Never mind. Luckily, I have enough skill in conversation for the both of us. "Say, I was going to grab some lunch. Want to join me?"

"Here?"

"Nah. I've seen the food coming out of that kitchen. I was thinking somewhere a little nicer. My treat," I add, in case the thought of the bill puts him off.

He's slow to answer. He even takes the first sip of his drink. It's done in an effort to disguise the fact that he's thinking hard about what to do, but it doesn't fool a pro like me.

"Yeah. Sure. Why not," he says eventually.

Praise the Devil! I down the last of my half-pint (*Old Peculiar* this time) and set the glass firmly on the table. "Did you want to finish your drink first, or are you ready to go?"

"No. I mean, yes, we can go."

Chapter Four

TOM

I still can't quite believe what's happening. I fear I may have dozed off in the pub and slipped into a dream. The guy from the bar—Saul—is stunning. He's so far out of my league, he's off the chart. Yet, I could have sworn that he was flirting with me earlier. That's why this must be an illusion, a fantasy. No one like Saul has ever made a pass at me in real life.

However, as we stand and prepare to depart, everything feels real. The battered, ancient wood of the tabletop is rough against my fingertips, grounding. My two glasses of cider remain all but untouched, confirming this is no alcohol-fuelled vision. Then there's the publican, whose expression I catch as we head towards the door. He looks surprised. That makes two of us.

Saul reaches the door first and holds it open for me. As I pass through the opening, I swear I can sense his fingers near the small of my back. He doesn't touch me; it's only the ghost of a presence, but it sends a shiver down my spine all the same. Fear or pleasure? I'm not certain. Maybe a little of both.

Outside, sounds seem louder than usual. Cars roar past, and the conversations of passersby are deafening. Saul lightly brushes my arm and indicates our direction with a nod. When he turns and pushes through the crowd, I blindly follow.

I don't know where we're going. For all I know, Saul could be a mass murderer and I his latest, hapless victim. I don't get that vibe from him. Nevertheless, I sense that he wants something from me, and if it's what I think it is, I'm inclined to give it. This is not the sort of thing I normally do; I've never hooked up with a stranger. Do I want to start now? What do I even know about this guy? But he's so gorgeous, and it's not like I'm committed...yet. I'll wait and see what happens.

As we continue on our route, however, I start to feel as if everyone is watching me, as if they know what I'm thinking, what I'm contemplating doing. (What I'm hoping to do.) We turn down a quieter side street and Saul drops back to walk alongside me, rather than leading the way. I'm suddenly aware of the sharp, immaculate press of his suit. It looks expensive, designer. I flush at the thought of my daggy attire and grip the hem of my T-shirt, making sure it's not caught up at the back. What about the jeans? I ease my hands into the pockets, checking for hitherto unnoticed holes, thankful when I don't find any.

Saul glances over and flashes me a breathtaking smile. His sleek, styled hair draws my gaze as he turns away and I experience another thrill of horror. I tug at my unruly curls several times, but they prove quite untameable and, barring a miracle, that's how they'll have to stay.

Another turn brings us back onto a main thoroughfare and I'm surprised when I recognise the locale. This is an upmarket neighbourhood—one I rarely frequent and in which I feel hopelessly out of place. Any lingering expectations of meeting a bloody end fade. I know I shouldn't judge safety solely by housing prices, but this does seem an unlikely spot for a vicious killing.

Saul slows his pace, and a moment later, I am staring at the imposing façade of an Italian restaurant. My unease returns. Did I completely misread the situation? Is this nothing but lunch after all? My disappointment is palpable. Obviously I wasn't as on the fence about having a casual sexual encounter as I'd assumed. Glancing at Saul as he opens yet another door for me, I experience a burst of longing that steals my breath. However, even that subsides when we enter and I take in my surroundings.

I've never set foot in a place like this. I'm not suitably attired. Panic sets in as I picture the utter humiliation of being denied service, of being sent packing with a look of disdain. But Saul is already speaking with the maître d' and then a waiter appears to lead us to our table.

Chapter Five

SAUL

Tom fidgets the entire way to the restaurant. We're walking along the street, just two blokes out for lunch, and he's shoving his hands in and out of his pockets and tugging at his T-shirt nonstop. He runs his fingers through those delightful blond curls so often I fear he'll have pulled them all out by the time we reach our destination.

Hey, it's nice to know I still have that effect on people. Always a great boost to the old ego. However, I'm certain some of the passersby have interpreted his erratic movement as a sign of mental instability. One woman definitely crossed to the other side of the street to avoid walking past him. Just saying.

By the time we make it to the restaurant even *I'm* relieved the journey's over. Nevertheless, there's nothing like splendour and sophistication to calm the mind, and this establishment has both in spades. A far cry from the pub we departed not ten minutes ago, this place is all crystal chandeliers and gleaming silverware, and the atmosphere soon produces the desired effect on Tom. Once he's seated, the table a meter-long barrier between us, he finally settles, restraining his actions to casting the occasional anxious glance around the room and gently fiddling with the cloth napkin. Oh yes, cloth. I only dine at the classiest establishments. No paper serviettes for this demon.

When we order, I notice that he picks the cheapest item on the menu, despite my insistence that the meal is my treat and he can have whatever he wants. I see the waiter raise a beautifully sculpted eyebrow when Tom orders a Coke to go with his Spaghetti Bolognese, but the man manages a polite, "Of course, sir," and seems mollified when I choose a suitably paired glass of wine to accompany my risotto.

"So, Tom," I say after the waiter struts away with our order, "tell me more about yourself."

"Like what?"

I pluck a dinner-suitable conversational topic from the vast array at my disposal. Something easy to start us off. "Favourite book?"

"Um. Well, I'm really more into comics."

My heart sinks. This might be harder than I thought. I try to keep up with the full spectrum of pop culture, but I doubt I know enough about DC and Marvel to maintain that kind of conversation for long.

"Sorry. You seem...cultured." He's tugging at his hair again. "I must come across as a bit of a nerd."

Oh yes! "Not at all." I flash him one of my most winning smiles, and he almost returns it...almost.

"I do like films," he offers, his expression hopeful.

Hmm, this I might be able to work with. "What's the last thing you watched?"

"*Guardians of the Galaxy II.*"

Then again, maybe not.

Chapter Six

TOM

Despair threatens to consume me once again. Saul seems right at home with fine dining and sophisticated conversation, but that's not my world. I dread to think what his impression of me must be. I know that I need to say something to salvage the situation. But what?

Luckily, the arrival of our main course saves me for the time being. I concentrate on winding the spaghetti around my fork, trying not to show myself up by splashing sauce everywhere. In this task, at least, I am successful.

As I set aside my cutlery, I glance up to find Saul's attention focused on the wall behind me. Instinctively, I twist in my seat and discover a reproduction artwork, hung in pride of place on the far wall.

When I turn back, Saul's gaze is now on me. My cheeks flush, but I manage to stammer, "Y-you l-like Waterhouse?"

I catch his surprise in the brief arch of his eyebrows; however, he quickly schools his expression. "I do. I've always been fond of both the Neo-Classicists and the Pre-Raphaelites. Waterhouse was pretty staid, but as for some of the others... You wouldn't believe the things that went on with those pretty models. What a wild time!"

I laugh. Saul talks as if he has personal experience, so I hazard a guess. "You know some artists?"

"Oh yes! I've known quite a few over the years. Always fun people to be around. Do you have a favourite?"

We spend a few minutes discussing artists and their different styles and techniques. For the first time, Saul and I find common ground, and that helps me relax. Nonetheless, a part of me remains on edge, wondering where this is going. For all the innocence of our conversation, every so often Saul's eyes meet mine, and there's something in his gaze that causes my heart to race. I still get the impression that this is not just lunch, that there's something more to it, and my emotions go into overdrive. Excitement. Longing. A hint of fear. Saul's done nothing obvious to account for the latter, yet I cannot brush it aside—a sense of wrongness. Perhaps it's just the surreal situation playing tricks on my mind.

The waiter comes to clear our plates and asks if we wish to peruse the dessert offerings. Saul responds that we do, and soon we're holding menus.

In truth, that was a big lunch for me and I'm pretty full. However, in case this *is* only a meal and nothing more, I want to draw out the encounter for as long as possible, so I review the options. It all sounds amazing...and expensive. Saul had said the meal was on him. Still, I don't want to be presumptuous.

I set down the menu. "What are you having?"

There's a mischievous glint in his eye when he meets my gaze. "I'm going for the Double Diablo Cake. You should join me."

I can't look away, and that now-familiar heat suffuses my cheeks once more. I wish I weren't so prone to blushing. Regardless of Saul's intentions in asking me here, he can be in no doubt of my attraction to him, what with my face flashing the information every two seconds.

My cock twitches and I will it to stay down. My humiliation will be complete if I have to stand at the end of the meal to reveal a raging hard-on, especially if Saul and I are to part ways once we finish dessert.

The waiter's return breaks our connection, offering me a momentary reprieve. Saul places our order, and the waiter departs. I ought to look away, to busy myself with some other object until dessert arrives. Such thoughts are in vain, however. I am unable to stop staring at Saul. If we do only have a few more minutes together, I want to memorise every line of his perfect face so that I can remember him once this is over. I don't want the recollection of today to fade too soon. I want to remember Saul for as long as possible.

Chapter Seven

SAUL

I glance over at Tom and am surprised to find him looking back at me. Praise Beelzebub! It's taken the whole meal but he can finally meet my eye without blushing or lowering his gaze. No, I take that back—there is some minor blushing—but it's still a good step forward.

Actually, the more time I spend with Tom, the more I like him. Under that nerdy crust lies a good sense of humour and a kind soul that makes him oddly angelic, especially when matched with that blond curly halo and those blue-gray eyes. I confess that there's a little corner of my hell-blackened heart that feels just the teensiest bit bad about what I'm trying to do to him. Hey, I said it's only a small part. Nothing I can't suppress; don't you worry.

The waiter returns and sets two plates in front of us. The opulent dessert is simply oozing chocolate. Like most demons, I have a terrible sweet tooth, so I dig right in. I'm probably shovelling the cake down faster than would be deemed suitable for polite society. But to hell with that! Within seconds I'm scraping the last vestiges onto my cake fork and licking hard to clean off every last morsel.

I can feel Tom's gaze on me, so I make the most of it and exaggerate the movement. I work that fork in and out of my mouth like I can't get enough, sucking hard. I conclude the display with a satisfied sigh and set the much-abused item of cutlery back on the plate.

When I glance up, Tom is stock-still. He was obviously about to take a bite when I began my show because his fork has come to a halt about an inch from his mouth. His elbow is locked in place and his—frankly quite perfect—lips are parted, jaw frozen open.

"Sorry," I say. "When I see something so delicious, I simply can't resist." I wink and rake my gaze over him.

Tom starts. He nearly drops the fork entirely but catches it just in time. The portion of cake is not so lucky. It tumbles off the metal prongs and lands on the tablecloth in a gooey heap.

The time is most definitely here. This one is ripe for the plucking.

I lean across the table, closing the distance between us. "Tell me, Tom, what would a night with me be worth to you?"

"What?"

He's confused, poor dear. And I don't really blame him—I've been using all my very best moves on him, after all. They'd be enough to floor even the most blasé of marks. For an innocent like this? Let's just say, I'll soon be scraping him off the floor the way I scraped that thick chocolate sauce off the plate.

"One night. With me. Doing anything you want, in as many ways as you want." I reach out and brush my fingertips against the back of his hand. He shivers. It's delightful.

"Hang on." He shakes his head. He's trying to focus. "Are you a...gigolo?"

Not a bad guess. I almost feel like one sometimes when I think of the things I've had to go through over the years to get a mark to put pen to paper.

"No, I'm not a gigolo."

At this point I'd usually say a few things to ease him in before the big reveal, yet the urge just to blurt out the truth and lay it all on the table overcomes my accustomed caution.

"Actually, I'm a demon. I procure souls and I'd like to acquire yours. Sign it over to me and I'll give you the best night of your life. That's a guarantee."

"You want my soul in exchange for...sex...with you?"

He's a smart cookie, this one. And I mean that as a compliment, not a snide aside. You'd be surprised how long it takes some people to cotton on to what I'm saying; Tom has nailed it straightaway. Hmm. The thought of nailing *him* makes my cock twitch. *Down boy. Not quite yet.*

"Yes. What do you say?"

He laughs. Okay, not the best response, but again, I've had worse. I keep my expression blank—no smile, no winking—and his laughter fades.

We stare at one another for a few moments. Then, to test the water, I briefly lower the illusion that masks my eyes, letting him glimpse the real me, the one behind this sexy exterior.

He gasps and sits back, keeping his gaze fixed on my face. "Why me?"

An intelligent question. Tom rises once more in my estimation. We passed the incredulous phase pretty quickly and efficiently. This could well be the easiest mark in a long time.

"You looked like someone who needed something." I could leave it there, but I feel compelled to add, "Plus, I find you appealing."

He nods. I can practically see the little cogs in his brain turning. "So, is this like in *Supernatural*? Do I get ten years or something?"

Now, *Supernatural* I *can* talk to. All demons watch that show. It's 'required reading' these days. If you aren't intimately familiar with that series, you look like an ass when a mark asks you a question about it. And trust me, a good eighty-five percent of them do bring it up.

"Way better than that," I say. "We wouldn't be so stingy as to set a time limit. No, you get to live out your natural life for as long as that may be. We don't interfere with your fate. All we ask is for the rights to your soul when the day comes. Whether that's in five years or fifty, it's all the same to us."

"And I'd go to Hell?"

"Yep. But it's really not as bad as you'd think. I mean, I live there myself when I'm not up here for work, and I'm none the worse for it. Some people rather enjoy the warm climate."

In truth, mortal souls and demons have wildly different experiences behind Hell's gates, and the heat is far more gruelling than a summer's day on a Mediterranean beach, but I see no need to go into those kinds of details at present. In cases such as this, less is usually more.

"What if I don't believe in Heaven or Hell?"

"Makes no difference to the contract." It's a fight to keep my expression neutral. Excitement builds, coiling in the pit of my stomach. However, the worst thing I could do at this delicate stage in the negotiations is let Tom see how much I want this. Time for my best poker face.

He gives me an assessing look. "And you really believe that a night with you is worth my soul? Think a lot of yourself, don't you?"

I grin. "I can *promise* you it'll be worth it." He's taken the bait. All that remains is to reel him in. "Or perhaps you aren't interested…"

I let my voice trail off and shrug, looking away, feigning indifference. Contrary to my words, I *know* Tom is interested. His pupils are like flying saucers. His eyes are so black that he almost looks like a *Supernatural* demon himself. If I were to slide my foot up his leg to his groin, I'd find him as hard as I am right now.

"Can I see this contract?"

I like a man who's straight to business. It means we can get to the fun part so much quicker. And the fun part is coming; I'm certain of that now. He's going to sign on the dotted line. The boss'll be happy, I'll be happy, and I'll make sure Tom gets a little slice of heaven tonight. It's the only taste he'll get of it, after all, once he's put pen to paper.

Some demons are all about filling their quota, and once they've gotten that signature, they no longer care. Me? I'm old-school. I believe in upholding my end of the bargain, and I make damn sure my customer gets what he or she has been promised. It's only fair; don't you agree?

I remove the parchment from the inner pocket of my jacket. Old-fashioned papyrus never fails to inspire the right level of awe and confidence. It's a simple document, just a few lines long, with none of the small print and incomprehensible clauses you see in television shows and films. We aren't out to swindle people. It's a business transaction, no more and no less, and in this business you want to make sure everything is clear and above board, to avoid the risk of any retractions at the last moment.

Tom takes the contract and scans it. He glances up at me and I nod: yes, that's all there is to it. He looks back down and reads it again. By the time he finishes, I have a writing implement in hand—a lovely Montblanc fountain pen, in case you were wondering—and when I offer it to him, he doesn't hesitate.

My heart rate quickens as he lowers the nib to the parchment. Time slows to a crawl as he forms the signature in long, drawn-out strokes. He adds the final flourish...and it's done.

Invisible to Tom, magic pulses through the parchment, sealing the deal. He sets the pen beside the contract and I reach across to take both, slipping them back into my pocket.

Tom's flushed and his breath comes quicker than before. "Um. So, what happens now? Do I see you at sunset?"

He's fiddling with the napkin again. It's down on his knee, but I can see what he's up to from the movement in his arm. Soon I'll give him something much better to do with those pretty pale fingers.

I pretend to consider the question for a moment, but actually I've already decided to give Tom a bonus. Yeah, okay, I confess, it's as much for myself as it is for him. But seriously, I'm so hard right now it's becoming painful. I don't recall ever having been this enthusiastic about fulfilling my end of the bargain before. It's certainly exhilarating.

"I know the contract says the night lasts from sunset to sunrise, but I have no other commitments today and we're already here together. How about I give you a few hours extra as a bonus? No additional cost to you, naturally." I throw him one of my most winning smiles. "I'll settle up with the waiter and then we'll get out of here."

Chapter Eight

TOM

With a knockout grin still in place, Saul rises, winks at me, and heads towards the front desk to hasten payment of our account. I remain pinned in place, heart and mind both racing. I can hear my too-fast breaths and try to slow my frantic gasps.

All along, I'd known Saul was different. I'd been certain he wanted something from me, and now I have my answer: Saul is a demon and he wants my soul. Has it, in fact.

A remaining nugget of incredulity in the back of my mind prompts that this is impossible, ridiculous. But what of those searing crimson eyes? A hallucination, my disbelief whispers. He could have slipped something into my Coke, drugged me. It's a legitimate suggestion. Yet I know, in my heart, it's false. This is no fantasy; this is absolutely real. I have signed away my soul in exchange for sex. I'm a walking cliché.

A pang cramps my stomach. Have I been too hasty? Have I made a terrible mistake? Then again, why am I worried? Saul said, and the contract confirmed, I won't be dragged to Hell any time soon. I will live out my life as nature, or God, if you prefer, intended. I've never been much of a believer, so what does it matter if I go to Hell at the end of it? It can't be that bad. Saul comes from there, and he hardly seems traumatised by his living conditions.

I look over at Saul, who is handing a card across the counter. I want him so badly that I fear I might die of need before we reach wherever it is we're going. Damn. What if that's his plan? If I die before we conclude our bargain, does that still count?

Saul saunters back to me and I force myself to my feet. I worry that my hard-on will be visible to everyone, but the thought is fleeting. Saul lightly brushes my arm as he guides me to the door. I'm nervous, more nervous than I've ever been, yet there's also something comforting about Saul's presence, his closeness. No one has ever focused on me so completely. That could just be a ploy—he's a salesman of sorts, after all—but I don't think so. Despite my throbbing anxiety (and throbbing body parts), talking with him, being with him, feels...natural. Maybe I'm simply seeing what I want to see, to reassure myself about the path I've taken. Honestly, I don't care. Perhaps this is wrong. But it feels right.

We leave the restaurant, and I follow Saul wordlessly down one bustling London street after another. My mind is too occupied to attempt conversation, and Saul seems to realise this as he makes no effort to engage me. Or perhaps it's simply that there *is* nothing to say. The deal is struck already.

The journey could have taken five minutes or five hours; I find it impossible to tell. Eventually, however, our pace slows and Saul halts in front of an imposing apartment building. He produces a key from his inner jacket pocket, and two minutes later, we are in a lift, heading up.

Somehow, reaching what I assume to be our final destination settles me. I no longer agonise over my choice. I know, if the situation arose again, I would do the same. Yes, I desire Saul physically, but it's more than that. He sees me, truly sees me, and to have that, even if only for a single night, is worth my soul without question.

The lift stops, the doors open, and we exit. At the end of the hallway, Saul opens a door and gestures me inside. I cross the threshold with a new set of fears. Do I have the courage to go through with this? And will I be able to avoid coming in my pants before Saul so much as touches me?

Chapter Nine

S AUL

I take Tom back to my place. Well, I say 'my place', but actually I share it with three other demons. It's a city apartment that the boss keeps available for us drones to use when we have overnight stays up top. Or for occasions such as this when we need somewhere to go to...fulfil our obligations.

I suppose it's nice in a modern, minimalist sort of way. If you like white and bland. The only plus point really is the bedroom. The king bed is utter luxury: all silk sheets and cushions, decorated in black, purple, and burgundy. Much more my colour palette than the rest of the apartment. The ceiling mirror can be used if needed. Not all customers are into that sort of thing, but I rather like it myself, so I'm hoping Tom won't object to a little self-voyeurism.

We've not yet made it that far though. I've left him seated on the white leather sofa while I move across the white carpet to procure two glasses and a bottle of bourbon from the (you've guessed it) white kitchen cupboards. I know some people like the plain look, but seriously, if I stay here for too long without a break, my eyes start to go funny. I don't know how people who live in these places full-time stop themselves from going blind.

I set my drink on the coffee table—which, in case you were wondering, is also white—and hand his to him. To my surprise, he immediately takes a sip. He was quiet on the way over and I begin to worry that he might back out. Not from the contract—nothing can change that now—but from the night ahead. In most situations, if a client chose to forfeit their payment I'd shrug and consider it an added bonus. (Not that it's ever happened in my experience.) However, the thought of missing out on making good on my end of the deal this time causes a tightening in my chest.

When did I fall so hard for this guy? At what time during the afternoon did it change from an emotionless business transaction to something more? I can't quite pin it down. And it's not just physical, either. Yeah, I know what you're thinking, and I'm not going to deny, that's a big part of it. I mean, the thought of getting my hands on that lithe form, running my fingers through those curls, and ploughing that no doubt tight ass has my cock straining against my clothing, desperate for release. But it's more than that. I want to know Tom on—Dare I say it?—a more spiritual level. Something about him draws me in. It's a new feeling for me, and it's both exhilarating and, if I'm honest, a little frightening in its intensity. It's not often you'll hear a demon say he finds anything frightening, but I'm a modern thinker and willing to embrace my emotional side, yada yada yada.

I slip out of my suit jacket—the contract is still in the pocket, ready to be lodged in the morning—and lay it over the arm of the chair before taking a seat beside him. Close beside him. Close enough that our knees touch. The liquor has brought tears to his eyes. They're red and watery in the half light of the room.

(The boss is a big fan of dimmer switches to create the right mood for this kind of thing. He puts a lot of thought into his work.)

I pick up my drink and take a sip. Then I set the glass back down and reach over to take his from him, placing it beside my own.

I can see the movement in his Adam's apple as he gulps. He doesn't know what to do with his hands now the glass is gone, so he grips his jeans, bunching the material in his fists. I place my hands over his, and he uncurls his fingers. I make my way slowly up his arms, as far as I can reach in my current position. Then I return to his hands, lifting them and placing one on my shoulder and one on my thigh.

"You can touch me, Tom. Anywhere and as much as you want. Tonight is your night. Whatever you want to do, we'll do."

He nods, but he doesn't move, and I can see that I'm going to need to kick-start things or we won't leave this sofa all night. At least he's not pulled away. He clearly wants to continue—he's just shy. I can understand that. I am pretty awe-inspiring.

I shift my angle and slowly lean in, giving him a chance to pull away if he wishes. He doesn't, so I press my mouth to his. I keep the kiss gentle at first, allowing him time to get used to the idea and respond. It doesn't take long before he murmurs and his lips part.

Making the most of the opportunity, I slip my tongue inside. And, oh, he is heavenly. Or, at least, he's what I imagine heavenly to be. I've never been to the 'other camp' in person, you understand, so this is all conjecture. He is sugar and spice and all things nice. I can taste the bourbon, mingled with the tomatoey sauce from our lunch, and a slight hint of something spicy. I'm not sure if the spice is from the Bolognese or if it's natural. Either way, it's as delicious as fresh honey straight from the hive.

I move a hand behind his neck to stabilise his head as I deepen the kiss. To my utter delight, he responds, moving his tongue against mine, exploring my mouth. I massage his shoulder with my other hand and he groans, tipping his head back farther.

The movement makes him flop down in the chair, his head coming to rest against the moulded leather. In a fluid movement, I shift to straddle him. Now, this is *much* better. From here I have access to all sorts of wonderful places: all the places I've been longing to explore for hours.

I run my hands lightly over his chest, brushing his nipples through the thin fabric of his T-shirt. I know if I lower my thighs, I'll rub against the erection that is clearly straining against his tight jeans. But not yet. It's still too soon for that.

His eyes are shut and his mouth is open in a beautiful O. He's worthy of a painting. Something by Rossetti. Or else Leonardo da Vinci. Those two men knew how to capture true passion in a brush stroke.

As much as I'm enjoying the moment, the sofa is really not well designed for this kind of activity. Not unless you're a contortionist. Time to move this party somewhere more appropriate.

I climb off him, and he opens his eyes. There's a flash of angst in his gaze. Perhaps he worries I'm calling a halt. He needn't be concerned; this is only a minor rest stop. He should enjoy it while he can. If I have my way, it's the only one he'll have between now and dawn.

He takes my proffered hand and I pull him up. Keeping our fingers entwined, I lead him across the room and open the bedroom door. The little exhalation of breath as he takes in the room in all its glory makes me smile.

I usher him to the bed and guide him down onto the cushions, climbing up after him. I almost laugh. He looks so out of place against the vibrant silks in his T-shirt and jeans. Better get them off him as soon as possible, do I hear you say? I absolutely agree.

I tug at the bottom of his T-shirt and he gets the message, raising his torso so I can pull the offending garment over his head. I toss it behind me, not caring where it lands as long as it's far from the bed. Whilst I'm not always averse to an audience, I don't really want a bunch of comic book superheroes watching. Oh, don't worry, you can stay. I wouldn't send you packing just as things are getting interesting. Not after you've come so far on this journey with me already, you sneaky little voyeur, you.

I return my attention to the task at hand and take a moment to admire the perfection laid out before me. Tom was hiding a damn fine body under that baggy T-shirt. He's no bodybuilder, but he's still nicely toned.

I run my hands over every inch of exposed skin and he shudders beneath me. I straddle him again so I can feel the vibrations of his body against my thighs. Every tremble sends a jolt of pleasure straight to my cock. I bend over and run my tongue across one pink nipple and then the other. They harden under my ministrations, and Tom murmurs my name.

Not only is it the first time he's spoken since we left the restaurant, it's also the first time he's said my name. I've always hated the sound of my name but, somehow, on his lips it has a different ring to it. I want to hear him say it again, and again, and again. I want him to whisper it in my ear and then scream it loud enough that people three streets away will hear.

I pinch his nipples between my thumbs and index fingers and he arches, lifting clear off the bed. Oh, he's a sight to behold, that's for sure. I quickly slip an arm behind his back and hold him up to whisper in his ear.

"Sweet Tom, I can do things to you that you've never thought of in your wildest dreams. I want you to writhe in pleasure on this bed all night. I can take the lead, but if you want anything, at any time, you must tell me. I'm like the proverbial genie in the bottle. Your wish is my command."

"I..."

"You don't have to be afraid to say anything here with me. Speak."

"I want to touch you too."

Ah, an easy request, and one with which I am more than happy to comply.

I lower him back into the cushions and undo the buttons on my shirt. I could rip them off and be done with it in a matter of seconds, but I look down and meet his gaze, taking my time. I drag out each button, until he's close to whimpering, before I shrug off the green shirt and let it fall to the floor.

He reaches for me and I pull him back up. Our bare chests press together, and we explore each other's arms and backs with eager hands. I massage my way down from left to right, moving from shoulder to hip, and he mirrors my every move. Even *I* start to lose focus, unsure where I end and he begins. Then I shift a little, and we both groan as our erections brush against each other.

I swing my leg back over, manoeuvring off him so I have more room to complete the long-overdue disrobing of his lower body. I work at his belt buckle, his button, and finally his zip, which I ease down slowly, drawing the moment out as long as I can. He's already lifting his hips and I ease the jeans down his legs. I yank off his trainers without worrying about the laces, and the socks and jeans follow.

Bending, I press my face into his groin, taking a moment to savour his musky smell. Then I lick him through his underwear, slathering my tongue over his hardness until the material of his briefs is wet through. He's practically humping into my face now, though I can tell he's trying to keep still.

I draw another whimper from him as I slip my fingers under the elastic. I ease the briefs down over his erection, along his legs, and send them off to the Land of Forgotten Clothes, otherwise known as the floor.

He's completely bare to me now and the sight is making me salivate. He's bigger than I would've expected, given his frame, cut, and already oozing pre-cum. Well, waste not want not as I always say.

I swoop down and lick the head, getting my first delicious taste of him as he bucks beneath me. He's gripping the cushions so tight that I'm pretty sure two at least are going to be mangled beyond repair by the end of the night. Not that I mind. They'll make a nice souvenir. One for each of us, perhaps.

I lean in again and lick from base to head, pressing firmly against his hardness with my tongue. As I reach the top, I take him fully into my mouth, gripping the base with my right hand and putting a little pressure on his hip with my arm, so he doesn't break my nose when he rears up.

I start a slow rhythm, sucking lightly and giving a gentle squeeze and tug with my hand. Gradually, I build the tempo, sucking harder, moving faster. Tom is writhing beneath me—just as I promised him he would—and he's babbling away under his breath. It's a little incoherent, but I can make out my name in there pretty regularly, and that's all I need to hear. I add a swirling motion with my tongue that has him thrusting into my face, and I have to steady his hips again with my free hand. Deciding to put him out of his misery, I hum. The extra vibration does the trick and he comes. He shoots his load down my throat and I swallow it all, sucking hard to get every last drop of nectar from him.

I sit back and look at him. His eyes are closed and his breathing is fast and shallow. His face and neck are flushed a beautiful shade of pink that looks well against his blond curls. I decide he should always look like this. It suits him. Someone should do this for him every morning, every hour if necessary, to keep him looking utterly debauched. Right now, you could mistake him for a Greek god.

My cock is so damn hard that I'm worried I could come just from looking at him, from seeing the results of my work so far. The thought of pushing up into him, impaling that beautiful body, is driving me to distraction. I have to force myself to remember that this is Tom's night. It will only happen if he wants it as well.

My little godling's eyes flutter open and he stares up at me. I can't resist the allure of those lips and crush him into a fierce kiss, which he mirrors, plundering my mouth with his honey tongue. We are both panting by the time we break away.

"Will you…" He pauses for one heartbeat, two, before he tries again. "I want you…inside me."

The words are music to my ears! It takes all my willpower not to come right then and there. I go to undo my trousers, eager finally to be freed from the confines of layers of material, but he sits up and brushes away my hands. He works at the fastenings with his nimble fingers, and soon I'm down to my boxers.

When he pulls those down, my cock springs free and, by Satan, it feels so devilishly good. It feels even better a moment later when he takes me in hand. He wipes his fingers over the head, using the pre-cum to lubricate as he settles into a steady rhythm.

I let him explore awhile but then ease him off. It's too much in my heightened state. Any more and it will be over before it's begun, which would be disappointing for both of us.

I shuffle across the mattress to the bedside table and open the top drawer. I remove the bottle of lubricant and crawl back to Tom. One of the perks of being a demon is that we're entirely immune to every disease and infection. As I told Tom on the way over, we can neither catch nor transmit any STDs and can, therefore, dispense with the prophylactics. Lubrication, though, is always a must.

I settle between Tom's legs and slick a finger. I rub back and forth over his entrance a few times before slipping the digit inside. As I press my finger in, Tom groans, and I wait a few beats to give him time to adjust before I start to work in and out.

I move slowly, adding a second finger and then a third. I stretch him carefully. My cock is longing to replace my fingers, but I won't act on that desire until I'm sure he's ready. I want him to enjoy this. I want him to scream my name in pleasure, not in pain, as I move within him.

"I'm ready." His voice is barely a whisper. His eyes stare up at me, wide and black.

I remove my fingers and smear more lubricant over my cock, coating my length from base to head. Then I position myself, hook his right leg over my arm, and push forward.

It's tight. It's so damned tight. For a moment, I fear it'll be too much for him, but then, with a slight *pop*, I'm in. I pause and give him a moment. He scrunched up his eyes as I breached him, but now he's relaxing again. He squeezes my arm, and that's all the confirmation I need.

I inch forward. It's a maddening pace, but I maintain it until I'm fully sheathed. Oh, and he feels so good! I've slept with a lot of people during the course of my long existence—some for work, some for pleasure—but it's never felt like this.

I start to move, still keeping a slow pace at first, easing nearly all the way out, back in again, and then out once more. Tom is looking up at me and I meet his gaze. As our eyes lock, I thrust in quicker than before. He moans. I pull out and adjust my angle, changing my grip on his leg. This time when I impale him, I know I've hit the sweet spot because he screams and presses his head back into the cushions.

"Faster. Harder. Saul. Please!"

Well, I don't need any more encouragement than that.

I hook his other leg and grip the backs of his thighs, pressing my fingers hard into the soft flesh to steady him as I ratchet up the pace. I am ploughing his ass now and it's mind-blowing. The friction is just right, and he's hugging me so tight, every little movement sends a shockwave of pleasure through me. It's complete sensory overload.

He reaches between us and grasps his cock, which is rock-hard again. He pumps in time to my thrusts, and it's so beautiful that I feel a sudden urge to claim him as mine. No one should touch his skin but me. No one else should be allowed inside him. It's a completely irrational thought and I've no idea from whence it came. But then I feel my climax nearing. The physical takes over from the mental. My rhythm becomes desperate and erratic.

Tom reaches his peak first. He screams my name as his cum sprays his chest, white on white. That's enough to push me over the edge, too, and I climax. I shoot my load into his perfect ass, and I swear, I've never come so hard or so long. For a moment I think it will never end, that I'll be coming inside him forever. But gradually the spasms recede and I slow to a stop.

I release Tom's legs and collapse on top of him, smearing his cum between us. We are both panting. When I can finally move again, I inch higher and kiss him, running my oil-slicked fingers through his hair and tugging lightly on the curls.

"That was...wow!"

"I aim to please."

I keep my tone light and jovial, but that's not how I'm feeling. Rather, I'm hit by the terrible realization that this night ceased having anything at all to do with work a long time ago. That's never happened to me before, and I'm worried where it will lead. For now, though, I have to concentrate on Tom. I *want* to concentrate on Tom. On his pleasure.

"Catch your breath, sweet one. We still have a long night ahead of us."

Chapter Ten

Tom

Saul is dozing at my side. I don't believe it's a full, deep slumber. Like me, he is temporarily overcome by our exertions. It's been hours. I still find it hard to fathom how many times I came. Maybe it was some form of magic because it certainly seems more often than is humanly possible. I'm utterly spent now though. My eyes are heavy, but I don't want to sleep. If I do, by the time I wake this will be over, and I want to hold on to the night for as long as possible.

I made the right decision with that contract. Of that I have no doubt. A lifetime in Heaven could not equal this. Saul didn't lie when he said that a night with him was worth my soul. Indeed, I'd gift it to him a second time were it possible. Not that I'll tell him so. He's far too cocky as it is. The heat of his bare skin against mine, the feeling of him moving inside me—these are memories I'll treasure forever. In those moments we were as one. With my previous partners it was only sex. With Saul, it was a union, a joining, not just of bodies but of hearts and minds. For me, anyway.

I glance at Saul, watching the gentle flutter of his eyelashes. Naturally, I'm not so naïve as to think this could have meant anything to him. To Saul, I am an assignment, nothing more. He played his part to perfection and gave me everything he promised, but I'm sure he's already contemplating his next job.

A chill sweeps through me at that thought, but I brush it aside. I'm a fool if I expect anything more. It was a wonderful night, but now it's over. Unless…

Saul is a businessman. Suppose I were to offer him a new deal? Would he accept? I tick over the possibilities, pondering the workability of various scenarios. I've already sold my soul to the devil, so what difference would another contract make? When he wakes, I'll put the idea to him and see what he says.

With that decided, and my sadness lightened as a result, I wriggle across the silky sheets and curl up against Saul. I can't help but loose a sigh at the way our bodies slot together as if we were made for one another. Saul's skin is warm, and a pleasurable shudder runs through me.

Tiredness beats down upon me, but I still don't want to give in to sleep. I fear that if I do, I'll wake to find Saul already gone, before I can share my proposition. No amount of willpower can hold back nature forever, though, and even as I rail against it, my eyes close and consciousness slips away.

Chapter Eleven

SAUL

I can sense the approaching dawn. Not in the way vampires can, before you ask. Coming from darkness, I can simply feel the build-up of light. The sun remains below the horizon for now, but it won't be long before the first rays break forth. Once that moment's here, the terms of the contract are fulfilled.

I look over at Tom. He's sleeping—exhausted, but I hope blissfully so—amidst the cushions. He's such a stark contrast to the dark silks. Light against the darkness. Light against *my* darkness. Oh Hell, since when did I become so bloody sentimental? What I should do is ease off this bed, get dressed, write him a note instructing him to shut the door on his way out, and then leave, never to see him again. Until I come to collect on our deal. Yes, that's absolutely what I should do. So why am I not doing it? Why am I sitting here waxing lyrical about the sunrise and the light? I chose darkness long ago, and Tom belongs to the light. It's as simple as that.

Except it isn't, is it? I've changed all that with my contract, my promises, and my seduction. Tom is pledged to the dark now, as surely as I am. And he'll start to feel it. There may not be a time limit on our contracts, but I wasn't entirely honest with him. Each passing year the darkness will take a firmer hold. He'll sense it—

maybe not straightaway but eventually—and there'll be nothing he can do.

Oh, don't look at me like that! I know, all right? I shouldn't have done it. I should've walked away, gone after another fish—they always say there're plenty in the sea, don't they?

But I didn't.

I said, don't look at me like that! What help were you? You could've said something. You could've tugged on my sleeve, told me to hold up. You're just as culpable as me, you know—you stayed for the show, after all. You wanted excitement, wanted to see me in action. You wanted to see him come undone every bit as much as I did. Don't deny it. The fall of the angelic geek with the golden locks. By all things unholy!

Wait a minute: the contract.

I carefully edge off the bed and scurry through to the lounge. My jacket is still draped over the chair, and when I reach into the pocket, I can feel the parchment. Normally I'd have lodged it before the ink was even dry. This time, I'd been so obsessed with getting Tom back here, I'd put off the admin until this morning.

What if I never lodge it? Would the boss know? I've always been good at the bureaucratic side of things. The thought of not lodging a contract has never occurred to me. Will it be enough? No, surely not. Even if Tom's not booked into the system, the magic of the contract will still draw him into darkness. Destroy the contract then. Is that even possible? Has anyone ever tried? I rack my brains, running back through the centuries. Mortals have tried to destroy contracts before to no avail, but I can't remember any occasion when a demon has attempted such a thing. Maybe, just maybe...

"Saul?"

I look up from my contemplations and see Tom in the doorway. He has wrapped a burgundy sheet about him and is rubbing his eyes with the back of his hand.

"Is it dawn?"

I swallow the lump in my throat. "Nearly."

All sorts of things are bubbling up in my mind—things I want to say to him—but I've not done anything like this before, never felt anything like this before, and I don't know where to start.

"I'd like to make a new deal. Is that possible?"

His question takes me by surprise and I don't have an answer ready. In the end, all I can muster is "What did you have in mind?"

"Give me ten years, like on the tele. Ten years and then you can have my soul."

"In exchange for…?" I ask the follow-up automatically, my mind still struggling to keep track of what's happening.

"You stay with me throughout that time. Not during the day—I know you'll have to work—but every night. If ten years is too much, we can make it five. Three, even."

I raise my hand to stop him. I don't mind confessing, I'm a little overwhelmed by his request. And touched. See, I told you I could channel my emotions—I truly am a twenty-first-century demon.

"No, Tom, no more contracts. I should never have made you sign the first one. I regret it." I can't meet his eyes. I have to look away.

"Hey, you didn't *make* me do anything. I weighed the offer and made my choice. It was of my own free will."

"But I seduced you."

I start when Tom's hand comes down on my shoulder. I hadn't even noticed him approach.

"I'm not quite as naïve as you seem to think, and you're not as irresistible as you'd like to believe, either."

"Hey!"

Tom holds up his hands and laughs. "Don't 'hey' me. I'm not saying you aren't awesome, or that last night wasn't the best I've ever known, but a little humility goes a long way."

"You'd really sign away the best years of your life for a few nights with me?"

Not that I'm accepting his request for more humility, I would have you know, but I do find it unbelievable that this sweet boy would give up decades of his existence just to be with little old *moi*. The thought leaves an unfamiliar yet deeply pleasant warmth in my chest.

"Yes, I would. I've never met anyone like you, Saul. And last night, being with you, felt more right than anything I've ever known."

"I know." The words slip out unbidden; however, as I hear them, I know them to be true. I may not understand these strange new sensations, but I can't deny their presence.

"You feel the same? Really?"

"Yes. But no more contracts. In fact, not even this one. Not if I can help it."

I pull the contract out of my jacket pocket and take it into the kitchen. Tom trails behind me, dragging the sheet in his wake. I open a white cupboard and pull out an equally white saucer, which I place on the white counter.

I drop the folded contract onto the saucer and focus my energy. I draw up the fire from Hell—Yeah, I can do that. Pretty cool, eh?—and concentrate it into the paper. The parchment bursts into flame and I watch it burn until all that's left is ash. Then I tip the remains into the sink, washing it down the drain.

"Will that actually work?"

There's a hopeful edge to Tom's voice that causes tightness in my chest.

"I hope so. I've never actually attempted anything like this before. Of course, it may just make the boss very angry, in which case we could find ourselves flung into a fiery pit, or on the run forever."

"Fiery pit or a life on the road. As long as I'm with you, either is fine by me."

I close the gap between us and pull him into my arms. Our kiss is fierce and desperate, and I try to throw into it all the sentiments for which I couldn't find words. I hope he gets the message. Romance has never been my strong suit, I confess. I've never had any call for it before, never needed anything beyond the basics of seduction and the pleasures of sex. But now a spark of light has come to life inside me and it's burning hotter than all the fires of Hell.

Something else has come to life too. Something not so much internal as external. And if the hardness pressing into my thigh is what I think it is, I'm not the only one experiencing this...animation.

I break the kiss and reach through a gap in his sheet cocoon to grasp something hot and pulsing and utterly mine. "Well, since there's a chance we'll be hunted down pretty soon, I feel it imperative we make good final use of that soft bed."

Tom grins and runs ahead of me, nearly tripping over the sheet in his excitement. I cast a final glance at the empty sink and then follow him.

Chapter Twelve

SAUL

Several Months Later

It's not easy being on the run. Sure, it looks exciting in all the films—action, adventure, amorous assignations—but that's a crock of shit. Well, maybe not the amorous assignations. We do have our fair share of those and no denying it. But as for the rest of it... In reality, a life on the run is tiring, dirty, and not the least bit soppily romantic. Tom and I are no Bonnie and Clyde—and perhaps we should be grateful for that.

We've been holed up in this nondescript—Or do I mean derelict?—hotel for three days now, neither of us having set so much as a single foot outside since we checked in. We order takeaway or room service when we need to eat, and the sign perpetually hanging from the door handle is clear for all to read: Do Not Disturb. Soon we'll have to move on again. The grace period seems to be five days. Any longer than that and we risk being picked up. The first place we went, we stayed for a week, and on the evening of the seventh day—ironic, I know— the boss sent us a visitor in the guise of a pizza delivery boy. It got *pretty* ugly. I mean, I could all but feel the flames kissing my soles as we hightailed it out of there.

Who'd have guessed it would come to this? When I singled Tom out, I'd planned on getting a signature for his soul, making good on my end of the bargain, and then moving swiftly along. How was I to know the strange effect that beautiful, innocent nerd in the Marvel T-shirt was going to have on me? My sweet Tom has a magic about him, that's for sure. I'd assumed I was the one weaving the spell over *him*, but one look into those clear baby blues, one brush of his fingertips on my bare skin, one press of his lips against mine, and I was a goner. Little old *moi*, demon deal-maker extraordinaire, professional to the eternally damned core was suddenly desperate to cast it all aside, to—Dare I say it?—repent of my actions and void a perfectly legitimate contract. Now here I am, fallen from Hell's grace and being hunted by my own kind, who took none too kindly to my ever-so-slight bending of the rules to save a veritable angel from the darkness. But, hey, it's not all bad news. I do have Tom at my side. And that makes it all worthwhile, believe me.

My clever trick with the contract worked. Go me! The blast of Hell-Fire destroyed the parchment good and proper—signature, magical binding, and all—and Tom's soul is officially off Hell's menu. Or rather it should be. I honestly don't know how things stand right now. It may depend on whether we get caught. I'm not up to speed with all the small print and legalities, but it seems our actions have ruffled more than a few feathers and scales. From what I could get out of Pizza Boy before I dry-roasted his arse back below, the boss is majorly pissed about my change of heart and has threatened to drag Tom to Hell, contract or no contract. Should the fiery legions of the damned get a hold of us, there's gonna be hell to pay, so I, for one, would prefer to stay firmly on the lam.

I tweak aside the lank, faded fabric masquerading as a curtain—I think, once upon a time in a magical faraway land, it *might* have been navy blue—and glance through the grimy pane of glass. What little I can see of the sky is still dark, only the barest tinge of a yellow-pink glow visible on the distant horizon. I release the material and it falls back into place, emitting a cloud of dust that hangs in the air for a moment before descending, snow-like, towards the ratty carpet. As I watch the particles land, a dubious stain in the corner of the room draws my gaze. Whatever it is—was—it appears to have eaten away half the strands of polyester, leaving a misshapen, threadbare splodge. I could bend down and give it a sniff, work out what caused the damage, but I'd rather not get that close. I know what you're thinking. Not the sort of squalor in which you'd expect to find a self-respecting demon like me living. Right? A few short months ago I'd have agreed with you. But things have changed.

With the boss on our tail, Tom and I must do what we can to survive. Our road trip started off rather more upmarket—five-star luxury in the Hilton, the Four Seasons, the Ritz—but I quickly cottoned on to the fact that we were being found much quicker in those places than when we went for something more in the budget range. Makes perfect sense when you think about it. Demons like luxury, so there'll always be greater numbers of them hanging around the classy establishments. More chances of being spotted and ratted out. This particular residence is especially vile, but it's not for too much longer. Last night marked the end of day five; it's time for us to pack up and move on.

This is the best time of day—or night, depending on your reasoning—to make our escape. At this hour, all but the die-hard clubbers amongst the humans are asleep, and demons are either busy fulfilling their part of any agreements if they sealed a deal, or getting a few hours' shut-eye before trying again on the morrow if they failed to secure a new contract. This is the optimum time for a well-known wanted couple like us to slip away unseen. I have the manoeuvre down to a fine art, and it always starts the same way: waking Tom. This is the single most time-consuming aspect of each escape. Packing our stuff, checking out, and journeying to a new abode—those things are easy. The first two are accomplished in a matter of minutes; the latter varies according to our destination and mode of transport, naturally. But waking Tom. Ah, that is another story. It's a task I truly, truly hate. And who could blame me. I mean, take a look at him...

I glance over at the bed where Tom lies in peaceful slumber. His face, framed by a halo of blond curls, is angled towards me. A gentle exhale makes several of those golden strands flutter. His full, oh-so-tempting lips are slightly parted, and for a brief moment I *do* want to wake him, so I can claim them in a kiss. He's only wearing boxers. We don't have an extensive wardrobe with us, and sleepwear was the last thing on our minds when we made our initial getaway. Actually, it's the last thing on our minds even now.

I permit myself a moment to appreciate the hypnotic rise and fall of that smooth, pale chest before allowing my gaze to wander lower, over the ever-enticing bulge at his groin and down his long, lithe legs. Mmm. I remember how it felt to have those luscious legs wrapped around me a few hours ago, his heels pressing glorious bruises into my buttocks as I thrust into that perfect, tight...

My cock twitches and I fight to regain my focus. Do you see now why waking Tom is such a problem? For one, he looks so angelic when he sleeps that it always seems a pity to disturb him. But at the same time, I only have to look at him to want him, and we really don't have time for that sort of thing when we're meant to be making a swift and silent exit from the scene.

I've never been one to deny myself sexual satisfaction. One of the perks of being a demon has always been the opportunity to fornicate to my heart's content without any fear of reprisal. But since I met Tom, my body seems to have gone into lust overdrive. Sometimes, honest to Satan, I just can't help myself and I have to have him, sneaky getaways be damned. However, since those occasions invariably end in a messy retreat, once escaping only by the skin of our teeth, I try to keep my libido in check whenever possible.

With a firm "Down, boy!" to my cock, I move away from the window and approach the bed. The room is the size of a matchbox, so I only need to take two short steps to reach my destination. I kneel on the bed and then inch closer to my sweet boy. I contemplate a gentle shake of his shoulder to rouse him, but those lips are too damn tempting, so I lean in to press my own to them.

Lo and behold, true love's kiss awakens my fairytale prince, just like in the stories of my youth. I know he's fully conscious when he snakes his tongue into my mouth and skims his fingers up my arm, gripping tight as he reaches my biceps. Even with sleep-stale breath, he tastes divine, and the whole moment is perfectly delectable. But I know where this will lead if I don't manage to keep a modicum of control, so I pull away.

"Morning, my sweet Tom," I say.

I retreat from the bed, putting some distance between myself and temptation. No easy feat for a demon like me, used to indulging his every desire, I can tell you!

"Time to go?" Tom asks.

His voice is still gravelly from sleep, and I try not to dwell on how sexy it sounds...or how I long to have him put that mouth and tongue to a better use than speech.

"I'm afraid so." I offer an apologetic shrug.

"Give me five minutes."

This is a familiar script—we say the exact same words every time—and as I watch Tom walk into the motel's excuse for an en suite (which allows insufficient room to swing a flea, let alone a cat, and I could probably find a flea or two around here with very little effort), I wonder, not for the first time, how much longer we can keep this up. I'm beginning to grow tired of the constant running, and no doubt Tom is, too, although he's not one to complain. How long do we have left before that weariness seeps into every fibre of our beings and infects our affection for each other? How long until it all becomes so dire we cease to remember what drove us to go on the run to begin with? What if there is no fairytale ending in store for us? What if these few stolen moments are all we get?

Oh, by Satan, when did I become so devilishly maudlin? Forget everything I just said; the boy and I, we're fine. If I had the chance to do it all over again, I wouldn't change a single goddamn thing. Hell, I'd destroy a hundred contracts, a thousand, for Tom's sake. The boss can chase us to the ends of the earth if he likes. Nothing is going to come between us. I wish I could say that that thought is enough to disperse *all* my doubts. Still, what's the point in worrying about ifs and maybes? For now, I have more pressing concerns—such as how many bedbugs are going to be hitching a ride when I pack our suitcase.

Chapter Thirteen

Tom

I shut the bathroom door behind me. It sticks and requires some coercion before it finally closes with a firm *click*. Through the paper-thin wall, I hear Saul moving about in the other room. He unzips the suitcase and a series of gentle *thuds* follows as he throws our meagre belongings back into our shared bag—an already-falling-apart knockoff we got for a tenner from a market stall before we fled London. For all that Saul presents a crisp and perfectly manicured exterior, never a stray speck of dust besmirching his designer suit, he is a slob when it comes to general tidiness. He thinks I don't notice, but I know he uses magic to remove the soiling and wrinkles from his garments, despite the fact that he's told me a thousand times he's limiting the use of his powers to help us avoid detection. My T-shirts, on the other hand, are creased almost beyond recognition from the way he tosses them into a heap when he packs, and some of the transfers are starting to peel around the edges.

At first, I wondered why he never offered to magically iron my clothes along with his own, but then I realised the truth: he likes me dishevelled. There's something about it that turns him on. Occasionally he calls me his angel, and I wonder if that doesn't somehow factor in. Does it appeal to him to imagine he's corrupting me? Does my looking ragged and unkempt bolster that fantasy? I could ask him. But I'm not sure he reflects on his own motivations enough to be able to give me an answer, and I don't want him to think I'm unhappy. No more than he already does, anyway.

I've felt the change. It's been coming on for a while now, but during the past week it has leached into the physical plane. I sense the hesitation in his kiss. Initially, I figured it was me, that he'd grown tired of me but was trapped in the relationship, given the circumstances in which we find ourselves. Yet he's shown no decrease in passion or desire, no alteration in his care of me, only this strange detachment. I worked my way to the answer. He's worried I'll come to regret the choice I made when I left that shiny white apartment with him the morning he burnt the contract. He fears that I'll wish I'd never met him, never signed that piece of parchment to begin with. As if I could! He may think of me as an angel, but I'm no naïve saint. I knew what I was getting into, both when I signed the contract and when I decided to run away with him. I'm not as fragile as he thinks; I need to make him see that. I could tell him, but that would be pointless—he'd never believe me.

I pick up my toothbrush and squeeze out a good dollop of red-white-and-blue toothpaste. This particular brand never fails to amuse me—it's oddly patriotic, but in a nonspecific kind of way. After all, the colours would work as well for Chile as they would for England. Or Iceland, or Russia, or the United States... Thinking of America and patriotism turns my focus to Marvel. Yeah, I know. But I can't help it. Since we went on the run, I've missed several editions of the various comic series I'd been reading. And of all the things I left behind, it's those I miss the most. I wonder what's been happening in each of the stories.

In an attempt to assuage my craving, I hum the stage-show song from *Captain America: The First Avenger* as I brush my teeth. The tune is mangled by the movement of the brush and the foam that clings to the roof of my mouth—I prefer to blame those two things than admit that I'm tone-deaf—but its familiarity is comforting all the same.

When I'm done, I rinse off the brush and place it in the toiletries bag Saul and I share. We don't have much aside from our toothbrushes and the half-empty tube of toothpaste: a plastic razor (in need of replacing before its dull blade slices off half my face—either Saul's hair and beard don't grow at all or he deals with them magically, like his suits), a tube of lubricant (four-fifths empty—I don't know what it says about us that we get through the lube faster than the toothpaste), and a pound-shop travel-sized hairbrush.

I take hold of the latter, tug out a handful of blond strands that have accumulated between its plastic bristles during the last few days, and raise it to my head. I watch my reflection in the tiny, cracked mirror as I run the brush through my hair. We've not had time to stop for a haircut in weeks and my curls now hang almost to my shoulders. I look like a blond Kit Harrington.

"You know nothing," I tell my reflection. My reflection smiles mockingly back at me.

I lay the brush inside the bag and zip everything up. I can no longer hear Saul moving beyond the door, so I assume he's ready and waiting to depart. I finish my morning ablutions and hurry back to the bedroom. When I toss Saul the toiletries bag, he chucks it atop the pile of clothes (jumbled, as expected) within the suitcase. Then he reaches around the back of the bag and pulls the zip, enclosing all our worldly possessions.

"Where are we heading?" I wander to the room's single, wobbly chair and gather my clothes. I pull my T-shirt over my head first and then step into my skinny jeans, tugging them up my legs, needing a wriggle and a squeeze when I reach my arse.

I ask Saul the same question every time we shift abodes. He's never once asked my opinion on where we should go, but that doesn't bother me. I'm happy to leave him in charge of such things. I trust he knows what he's doing better than I would, and that there's some method behind our to-ing and fro-ing. At the rate we're going, I expect we'll soon be the most well-travelled pair in the whole of the British Isles. Perhaps we should lodge our endeavour with the *Guinness Book of Records*.

"Paris."

I pause, jeans still unbuttoned, and look up in surprise. We've been from Southampton to the Scottish Highlands and back again in the last few months, but we've never left the country before.

"I thought it was time to try a new tactic to throw them off our trail," Saul adds when I meet his gaze.

I finish fastening my jeans and glance at the rickety chair. Deciding not to risk it, I perch on the edge of the bed to put on my socks and trainers. "What about flight records? Won't they be monitoring such things? Won't they know where we've gone? I don't even have my passport with me, Saul. We'd have to go to my flat."

My flat. Is it even mine anymore? I'd paid several months' rent in advance, but the next quarter would have fallen due about a week ago. Has the landlord come knocking yet? Have they gone inside and found a fridge full of rancid milk and moulding food, my clothing still in the wardrobe, and no sign of a struggle to account for my absence? Have my work colleagues reported me as missing? Are there posters bearing a bad, ten-year-old photo of me gracing central London's street corners and shop windows?

The morning Saul destroyed the contract, he and I went back to bed and stayed there for several hours. It was midday when the first sign of trouble appeared in the form of an aged demon who wandered in on us, demanding we appear before some committee or other. Saul apparently didn't like the sound of that because the moment our visitor left he had us up, dressed, and hightailing it out of there. We didn't have time to plan, to make arrangements; it was an impromptu dash out of the city, first on foot and then by train. We ditched my mobile and my credit cards—luckily, Saul seems to have an inexhaustible (I assume magical) supply of cash—and I haven't been within five miles of either my office or my flat since that day. I have no idea as to the current status of my disappearance. I imagine that they must think I'm dead. Assuming anyone has noticed I'm gone. I have no immediate family to speak of and my only friends were my co-workers and people on social media.

I break off my contemplations and look up in time to see Saul shaking his head.

"Leave that to me, sweet Tom. You trust me, don't you?" He gives me one of his most winning smiles—the ones I can never resist, never say no to.

"You know I do," I reply as I stand and walk over to him.

We've lived in each other's pockets for nearly four months now, yet I'm still blown away every time I look at Saul. I could gaze at him for hours and never be bored. I know every line of his face, from the chiselled cheekbones to the luscious lips, from those effulgent emerald eyes to the silky sable strands of his hair. I know his catalogue of laughs and smiles—one for every occasion—his wry sense of humour, and his propensity to hide his emotions beneath a mask of self-mockery. To my mind, and to my enraptured heart, he is utter perfection. I still have to pinch myself when I think that he chose *me*. And I don't intend to waste a single moment of whatever time we have.

Believe me, I'm under no illusions. Even if we somehow stay ahead of our pursuers, our time together still has an expiration date. I'm a mere human, after all, and he is... Well, I'm not entirely sure how it works with demons, but from what I've picked up when I can persuade him to talk about it, he's pretty much immortal. However, I don't want to think about any of that right now, and I know one sure way to push such thoughts from my mind, at least for a little while.

I place my hands on his shoulders and stretch up to kiss him. His lips are warm and soft and as delicious as always. He returns the kiss and wraps his arms around me, tugging me closer. I rub against him, feeling the press of his hardness, creating a delightful friction. He groans. Then he pushes me away, slowly but firmly.

"Keep that up and we'll be getting back into bed." Saul runs his hand through his hair and I follow the movement, thinking about where else I'd like those long, skilful fingers to slide. "Later, Tom," he adds, seeing the line of my gaze. "You know what happens when we delay. But you are so damn tempting that I may just decide to risk it." He inches forward.

"No, you're right." I pick up the bag before I can change my mind. "You can romance me when we get to Paris. It's the City of Love, after all."

Saul laughs. "That it is. Come on, then. Let's make a move while we have the chance. The sooner we get there, the sooner I can do unspeakable things to you."

"Unspeakable?" My cock gives a twitch of interest at Saul's words—just as he knew it would. Oh, I'm not fooled by that innocent expression he's wearing; I can see the gleam in his eye. He's winding me up on purpose and I can already tell that it's going to be a long trip.

"Well, maybe not unspeakable, but certainly nothing that can be said aloud in polite company." He offers me a wicked grin; then he leans in and whispers in my ear.

A moment later, face flushed and cock pressing painfully against the zipper of my jeans, I amend my earlier statement: it's going to be a *very* long trip.

Chapter Fourteen

BARUCHIEL

Baruchiel made his way down the well-trodden path. The stones scorched the soles of his bare feet, and he contemplated the pain all those who passed this way surely felt. It wasn't just the heat—although that was bad enough—it was the sense of desolation that hung in the air. He could almost taste the bitterness, the despair, every time he inhaled. He'd never had cause to come this far below ground before. In fact, this was the first time in untold years he'd set foot outside the gates of Heaven. Once, he'd made regular trips between Heaven and Earth, acting as liaison officer whenever things got dicey with human–angel relations. His role had been to combat strife and restore accord, but these days humans were no longer willing to listen, the angels had given up trying, and his post had become obsolete. For centuries now he'd been on menial duties, passing the time as best he could. Until yesterday, when he'd received new instructions. He reached into his robes and withdrew the message, reading it yet again, certain he must have misunderstood. But, no, the meaning was clear, blunt even.

Journey to Hell STOP Diplomatic situation STOP Reclaim soul Thomas Ives STOP Do not fail STOP

Baruchiel replaced the piece of paper in his pocket and continued on. Ahead, he could see the gates. As he drew closer, Baruchiel noticed someone had scrawled a message in black marker on one of the gateposts: Abandon hope all you jerks who have your scrawny arses dragged thru here. Below, someone had added in green felt-tip pen Or your fat asses, suckers. It wasn't exactly Dante, but Baruchiel supposed it was close enough. And the sentiment behind the statement was all too true, in spite of the misspelling and the inelegance of the prose.

A heavy clang made Baruchiel start and he looked up to see the gates scraping open. The sound was akin to nails being run down a blackboard and Baruchiel couldn't repress a shudder. A moment later, a rather hirsute demon poked his head through the opening, his gleeful smile turning to a frown when his gaze fell on Baruchiel.

"An angel? Whatcha think you're doing down 'ere, pretty boy? I'd clear off sharpish if I were you, before the boss gets wind of it. 'E's none too 'appy with you fluffy-winged lot on 'igh at present."

The demon started to grind the gates closed, so Baruchiel sprinted forward and thrust his foot into the opening.

"I am well aware of that. In fact, it is why I am here. I have been sent to negotiate."

"Negotiate, eh?" The demon rubbed his chin, his fingers disappearing into his bushy beard. "Well, I guess it'd speed things up a bit 'aving one of you on 'and. No need to wait for the useless inter-realm mail service. The sooner we clear all this up, the sooner the boss'll be off our bleeding backs. Well, I s'pose you'd better come in."

As soon as the gap was wide enough, Baruchiel squeezed through, and the gates slammed shut behind him. It was a disconcertingly final sound, and had Baruchiel not known he was guaranteed egress upon completion of his mission, he might have felt uneasy.

"Come on, then," the demon said, turning his back on Baruchiel and plodding away. "You'd best come with me and meet Adramelech. 'E's the one 'andling this case."

Baruchiel followed the demon down a winding pathway. The temperature had risen dramatically, and if angels had been capable of sweating, Baruchiel was sure he'd be dripping buckets already. How in Heaven did the unfortunate mortal souls who ended their days here stand it? Then again, he supposed that was the point. You didn't wind up falling into Hell unless you deserved some kind of punishment...or had made an extremely dodgy deal.

On a visual level, the realm appeared deserted. They were the only two walking the path and Baruchiel saw no one in the distance. He could hear them though. The air rang with screams and sobs. It was a discordant music that blended into the background most of the time, so constant you ceased to notice it. But then someone would release a particularly loud moan or a high-pitched shriek and the plaintive, wretched sound would stab at Baruchiel's heart, making him miss a breath. He found himself wondering where they were, these poor, lost souls. What nightmare existence did they inhabit? What horrors were they forced to endure?

"'Ere we are then."

Baruchiel had been so lost in his thoughts that he'd failed to notice when the path straightened and became a road. Looking up, he was surprised to see that stone had replaced the barren landscape of earlier. Walls of rock towered above him on both sides, with makeshift rooms—dark recesses drenched in shadow—hewn into their surface. The work was haphazard, leaving jagged, vicious-looking edges around each uneven doorway.

"Adramelech! Visitor!"

The shadows within the nearest doorway shifted and a figure stepped out of the gloom. His upper body was that of a man, but his legs were those of a mule. Peacock feathers erupted in a fan from his lower back; however, a layer of ash obscured their bright colours. Baruchiel felt a tremor of revulsion that almost saw him take a step back, but he overcame the urge and held his ground.

Adramelech looked Baruchiel up and down with a sneer. "What do you want, angel?" He spat on the ground near Baruchiel's feet. On Adramelech's lips, the word 'angel' sounded akin to 'scum'.

Baruchiel glanced around, but the demon who'd brought him here had vanished. *Looks like I am on my own, then.* "You are Adramelech?" The demon nodded and Baruchiel continued. "I have been told that you are the one with whom I should speak regarding the soul of one Thomas Ives."

Adramelech's eyes flashed crimson and a smile spread across his face. "Ah, Thomas Ives. This is by far the most interesting case I've had in years. Clear-cut all the same. The boy's soul belongs to us."

Baruchiel frowned. "It would appear that Heaven does not agree with that assertion. Otherwise, they would not have sent me here."

"It's an internal matter and you lot upstairs have no right to interfere. No right at all."

"Internal? How so?"

Adramelech leant against the doorway, either managing to avoid the sharp splinters of rock or unfazed by them. "Didn't they explain the situation to you before they sent you down here?" When Baruchiel shook his head, he sighed. "By Hell! At least it's good to know that it's not just down here that workers are expected to complete their jobs without proper instruction. The things we have to deal with. The lack of savvy from management is shocking sometimes. Anyone would be pissed off. Look, the situation is this: Thomas Ives signed a contract. He was not coerced, the deal was made fair and square and everything played out well within the agreed rules. Due to an...unexpected event, the actual *physical* copy of the contract was destroyed. But that shouldn't make the agreement any less binding. A deal is still a deal, contract or no contract."

Baruchiel's interest in the mission commenced a brisk upward trajectory, for all his attempt at nonchalance. "I thought Hell's contracts were indestructible, impervious to mortal tampering once signed."

"It wasn't Thomas Ives who set fire to the parchment; it was one of our own. Like I said, it's an internal matter."

Adramelech seemed uneasy, almost hesitant. If everything were as above board as he claimed, why would Heaven interfere? And Baruchiel knew he had heard Adramelech's name mentioned before. He was no minor demon but a figure of some import, meaning this case was not your everyday bureaucratic mix-up. There was something else going on here, and Baruchiel intended to get to the bottom of it.

"Why would a demon break his own contract?"

"Sir! Sir!" A young fire demon dashed towards them, grinding to a halt in a storm of pebbles and soot. "They've been sighted."

Adramelech waved away the minion and turned to Baruchiel. "It's probably easier if you come with me so I can *show* you what's going on. Then you can return upstairs where you belong and leave us to our business."

Chapter Fifteen

SAUL

I fumble with the key card and make a fourth attempt to open the door. The LED on the panel remains persistently red. There's a puff of warm breath against my neck as Tom leans over and plucks the plastic rectangle from my hand. He inserts it into the slot, and a second later, there's an electronic hum, the light turns green, and I'm able to depress the handle. Yeah, yeah. Don't think I don't sense you grinning behind my back! I got it warmed up for him. Everyone knows these things never work on the first few tries. I'm sure some smart cookie somewhere—probably in Germany or Russia—has already conducted a scientific experiment and proven it. I'd look it up on Google and share the results with you, but I don't have the time right now. On the run, remember?

We enter the room and it's a pleasant surprise. This place was only listed as mid-range accommodation— Satan forgive me, I simply couldn't stand another hideous budget motel—nevertheless it's fairly cosy and a damn sight cleaner than the last few places in which we've had the profound misfortune to crash. The walls are bright and unstained (no hint of peeling paintwork); there are no funky smells coming from the bathroom (which, though small, appears well maintained); and when I sit on the edge of the double bed (a real one, not two singles pushed together), the mattress is firm and both lump- and squeak-free.

Tom sets our bag down on the chair and wanders to the room's single window. When he pulls aside the curtain, I see that we've even lucked out in this area and done better than the brick walls of recent weeks. Sure, it's not a view of the Eiffel Tower or Notre Dame, but we are at least overlooking the street. The neon lights of Pigalle flicker on the other side of the pane, and when I stop and listen, I can hear the rush of traffic and the murmur of voices from the pavement two stories below.

Our journey here was pretty uneventful. As far as I can tell, we quit the hotel, and then the country, unobserved. When the train pulled into the Gare du Nord, I hailed a taxi and instructed the driver to take us on a circuitous route around the city before proceeding to our hotel, just in case we'd picked up a tail. The Armenian taxi driver enjoyed himself to no end—said he felt like James Bond— and a generous tip bought his silence, on the off chance anyone questions him about his fare. Hey, I've watched plenty of detective movies and film noir in my time and I know how to cover my tracks. Of all aspects of our life on the run, the dodging and weaving, showing off my superior cunning is probably the best bit. I let my gaze wander from Tom's curls, down his back to his pert arse. On reflection, make that the second-best bit.

Tight denim currently hugs the object of my attention. The material clings to Tom's flesh like it can't get enough—Who could blame it?—and I feel a sharp stab of jealousy. Time to show that fabric who owns that delicious rump!

I slink forward just as Tom lets the curtain drop. Before he can turn, I snake my arms around his waist and pin him to my chest. His breath hitches as I grind my already-half-hard cock against his arse.

"I promised you unspeakable things," I whisper.

I bite gently on his earlobe, sucking the fleshy nub into my mouth as I ease my hands over his torso. His nipples harden at the persistent brush of my fingertips and then I skim lower, past his abs, lifting his T-shirt as I go. When I reach the waistband of his jeans, I squeeze the tips of my fingers inside, pressing ever downward, and Tom moans, dropping his head back onto my shoulder. Time to move this somewhere more comfortable.

I whirl him around in my arms and all but hurl him at the bed. He lands on his back and I am already on him, tugging that ugly T-shirt—Where does he keep finding these things?—up and over his head. He raises his arms to assist me and soon it's gone, leaving me with free access to his upper half. I swoop down on his nipples and alternate lapping my tongue and scraping my teeth over each in turn until he's writhing beneath me. Then I fasten my mouth just above his collarbone—a spot I've discovered is *wonderfully* sensitive—and I suck...hard. Tom makes an adorable yet utterly unintelligible gurgling sound and I glory in a job well done. I sit back for a moment to view my work so far. Tom's cheeks are flushed, his breath laboured, his pupils huge black discs, and the spot where I sucked is *definitely* going to leave a hickey. It's perfect. He's perfect.

He's watching me, waiting, so I make a show of removing my own shirt. Slowly. One. Button. At. A. Time. He thrusts his pelvis upward, seeking friction, but he should know better than that by now. He may have won his way into my hell-blackened heart, but in the bedroom, *I'm* the one in charge, and if he attempts to move things faster, I will respond by slowing to a snail's pace. I settle more heavily on his legs, preventing any movement on his part, and cut my unbuttoning speed in half. His lips part, he darts out his tongue to moisten them, and I feel his cock twitch against my thigh. Although Tom does sometimes try to gain supremacy in our little games, he never pushes for it *that* intently. In his heart of hearts, he likes to submit. And I like to *have* him submit to me, so it works out well for us both.

Finally done with the buttons, I let the shirt slide off my arms and then I shift back to the edge of the bed and lower my head to his crotch. I lick back and forth over the bulge in his jeans until he's bucking up against me. When he reaches to undo the button and pull down the zipper, I consider stopping him, dragging it out, making him beg. But I change my mind and allow him to free himself from the confines of his remaining clothing. It's to my own benefit, too, since I'm feeling rather impatient myself today. When the jeans are off, I toss them onto the floor— Take that, denim! I told you he was mine!—and return to the oh-so-pleasant task of making Tom squirm.

I run my tongue up his length once, twice, three times and then take him into my mouth. When he groans, I reach up and slip three fingers between his parted lips, encouraging him to suck on the digits as I suck on him. Once his saliva starts to drip down my palm, I let him slip from my mouth. A moment later, I have one of his legs balanced on my shoulder as I work a finger into him. I open him slowly and gently, adding a second digit and then a third, until he's stretched and ready.

"On your knees, sweet Tom. You may want to hold on to the headboard."

Tom scrambles to comply. As he moves, I see the pre-cum oozing from his cock. I lick my lips, and for a second, I'm torn. Part of me would like to taste him, to have him come in my mouth and then to thrust into him as he rides out his last waves of bliss. But the idea of making him climax *with* me wins out and I wait while he assumes the requested position.

I pull the single-use packet of lubricant from my trouser pocket. What can I say? I like to be prepared. And with Tom around, I need to be prepared twenty-four seven, seeing as how I desire him every waking moment. Hell, even when I'm asleep. He's all I dream about these days.

I remove my trousers, draping them over the back of the chair. Then I tear open the foil and smear the contents over my cock as quickly and efficiently as I can. Tom's gorgeous arse is right there before me and I don't want to waste a single moment. I want in.

I breach him in a single stroke, sheathing myself to the hilt, and we both groan. I wait a few seconds, giving him time to adjust, but soon I can't hold back any longer. I grip his hips, pressing my fingers hard into that soft flesh, and then I start to move. Sometimes we make love, slow and gentle; other days we fuck, hard and fast. Today definitely falls into the latter category. I set quite a pace, pulling him back onto me as much as I'm thrusting into him. Luckily, Tom followed my instructions and is keeping a firm grasp on the headboard, which is—so far— holding up under the assault. Should he let go of his anchor, I'm certain we'd both end up in a heap on the floor, like our discarded clothing.

By Hell, he feels so good. He always does. Tight and warm and...mine. Nobody else gets to touch him like this.

That thought adds urgency to my movements and my thrusts grow more erratic as I reach around his body and take his cock in hand. It only requires a few pumps before I feel him tense around me. The added squeeze sends me over the edge, too, and we come together, screaming each other's name. We collapse side by side on top of the crumpled sheets, our breaths ragged and loud.

I can hear the noise outside again. I know it never went away, but I was so lost in Tom, in our coupling, that it seemed as if the world beyond this room stopped while we were joined, only starting again once it was over.

I grasp Tom's arm, pulling him closer. He curls against me, his back pressed to my chest, and I know that all this—the running, the danger, the risk—is worth it. I made the right decision that night, and I care about nothing except enjoying what the two of us have...for as long as it lasts.

Chapter Sixteen

Tom

I let the towel fall to the ground and reach for my clothes. The water is still running in the compact en suite. One thing I've learned over the last few months of living with Saul is that he takes his showering seriously. His average shower duration is a whopping twenty-five full minutes. Sometimes it's possible to get him out in as little as fifteen, but a feat like that can be accomplished only with the lure of sex, which then results in a second shower. Oh yes, the love of my life is *obsessed* with cleanliness. His own, anyway.

I can't help but wonder whether it isn't because his home is a world of smoke and ash and heat. Must get pretty damn uncomfortable to be constantly battling sweltering temperatures, covered in a layer of brimstone. The feel of cool, clean water splashing over his skin has to be a wonderful change. I tried to ask him about life in Hell once—its inhabitants, their routine, what it was like for the souls that went there—but he shut down on me, his face turning deathly pale. Without meeting my eye, he assured me that it was something I would never have to experience, and then he clammed up completely. He sat in the chair, brooding and sporting a full-on Byronic pout, and I couldn't get a single word out of him for the rest of the evening. He didn't even try to ravish me when we turned out the light. So, I learned it was a topic to avoid. After all, I like being ravished.

Fully attired once more—for now, at least; you never can tell how long *that* will last with Saul around—I wander to the window and push aside the curtain. The sun set a good long time ago and the world outside is a wonderland of neon lights filling a dark, almost pitch-black sky. For some reason, I find myself remembering the opening shots from *Blade Runner*. Gosh, I haven't watched that movie in an age! If only I had my DVD collection with me...

A pipe judders, the water noise ceases, and a couple of minutes later, the bathroom door opens with a soft *click*. I don't turn, but I can hear the gentle pad of feet as Saul approaches. Hard to tell what mood he's in. Sex tonight was urgent, almost desperate, as if we were trying to hang on to something that is slowly slipping away. Based on past experience, the rest of the evening could go one of two ways. Either we'll spend the whole night fucking until we can't move another muscle, collapse exhausted, and wake sore and stiff limbed, our bodies still entwined in configurations that would dazzle even a professional contortionist, or he'll want to go out, leaving me alone in the hotel room. Sometimes he disappears for two or three hours and returns without a single word as to where he's been. I don't question him. I never doubt he'll come back for me, and I have no fears he's gone off with another. I'm not the jealous type, and even if I were, I'd have no qualms about trusting Saul. I know he's dedicated to me, heart and soul, as I am to him. Occasionally he needs his space for a while, is all, and it gives me the chance to gather my thoughts too.

Saul runs his fingers over my biceps. His skin is still clammy from the shower and goosebumps rise on my arm. "I'm going out for a bit."

I nod my understanding; there's nothing else to say.

His hand stills. "Would you like to come with me?"

Well, this is new. First Paris and now this. I turn and look into his stunning green eyes, unsure how I should reply. Is this some kind of test? Is he trying to work out how I feel about these side trips of his? What is the correct answer? What is he expecting—wanting—to hear?

"You said you wished to see Paris," he adds when I don't immediately respond. "I don't know how long our Channel-hop will remain undetected, so this could be the only chance we get to go outside before we move on."

"Yeah. Sure," I say, finding my voice at last. "I'd like that."

He gives a wide smile and any tension at this change in our routine dissolves.

I dash to retrieve my trainers from the floor, settling on the mattress to pull them on. To my left, I catch the occasional movement in the corner of my eye as Saul dresses. I know that when I turn around he'll be exquisitely suited, looking every bit the dapper man about town. I sometimes wonder what people think when they see us together—him so suave and sophisticated and me so...not. He's never commented on it, never once asked me to don a suit, to dress more formally. That said, I know he's not fond of my T-shirts. They're nearly always the first thing to go when he undresses me, and he's not averse to ripping them—'accidentally', of course—when he yanks them over my head. But he's never asked me to stop wearing them. Perhaps that says a lot about our relationship, about his feelings for me. Or maybe I'm reading too much into it.

Laces fastened, I stand and turn towards him. The slight catch in my breath is a common occurrence. So much so that I barely notice it anymore. I do notice *him* though. God, he's so beautiful. He's wearing his favourite green shirt. The colour of the fabric highlights his eyes, lending them an ethereal glow. It's the same shirt he was wearing the day we met, and I wonder if that's a coincidence or by design. Remembering our first, earth-shattering night rolling in burgundy silks and soft pillows, I feel a stirring in my groin. But I do my level best to ignore it.

The thought of saying, "To hell with Paris!" and getting Saul back into bed with me is tempting, yet my desire to see the City of Light wins out. Not to mention the fact that this will be the first time we've done anything together aside from sex and moving between accommodations. A stroll around the city is as close a thing to a date as we've managed so far, and I don't want to waste the opportunity for a little romance, a little blessed normality. I take a deep breath and get my libido under control. There will be plenty of time for bedroom antics later. For now, Paris awaits.

Saul's smirk tells me he noticed my indecision. I stick my tongue out at him in response. He arches a sculpted eyebrow in mock surprise and then slowly and obscenely licks his lips. Damn, if that isn't nearly enough to make me change my mind. But I'm not going to fall for his tricks. Not this time. I set my jaw and march across the room, grabbing the key card from the slot as I jerk open the door. Saul chuckles, but I sense him following, and I slip the key card into my back pocket as he pulls the door shut behind us.

We walk the streets arm in arm. The roads around Pigalle are bustling despite the lateness of the hour. Sex shops and clubs beckon us with flashing neon bulbs and pounding music—And there's the Moulin Rouge itself!—but we ignore them all and make our way along the Boulevard de Clichy, past Parc Monceau. The streets grow quieter as we travel away from Montmartre. We stroll together in companionable silence, and I take in as much as I can, flicking my hungry gaze from left to right, trying to match the scenes before me with the Paris of my imagination. The city has a somewhat disconsolate feel in these early hours of the morning, but I picture it by day: people laden with bags, moving from shop to shop; traffic vying for right of way, horns honking; the sunlight glittering over the rooftops. And, yes, it's every bit as enticing, romantic, and chic as I could wish.

But all the marvels of the city are eclipsed by the gentle press of Saul's arm against mine. To be able to walk with him like a normal couple brings me a rush of bliss. How I wish it could be like this every day. I can picture it: how we'd go to the movies, take long strolls in the park. Even shopping for groceries together would be wonderful. Will we be able to have that one day? I decide I'd rather not know the answer, and I brush aside such thoughts and return my attention to the world around me.

We reach the Jardins du Trocadéro—Don't be too impressed; I simply read the signage as we arrived—and there, across the way, is the Eiffel Tower, lit up like a Christmas tree by thousands of tiny bulbs, a beacon in the darkness. Hand in hand, we stroll onto the bridge, stopping midway to gaze at the city's greatest icon as the waters of the Seine slosh below us and a slight breeze ruffles our hair.

"Romantic enough for you?"

I glance over and see Saul examining his nails. It's a good attempt at nonchalance, but he forgets that I know him too well now, that I can tell the difference between his real emotions and the masks he dons either for fun or self-preservation. This one is clearly for fun and I'm tempted to let him win the charade. I almost confess; I come close to telling him that it's perfect, that it's everything I wanted. But that would be letting him off *way* too lightly. Instead, I shrug and assume my own indifferent pose.

"It's a start," I tell him, turning away so he can't see the smile tugging at my lips.

"What more do you need?"

He releases my hand and runs his fingers down my back. By the time he reaches my arse and squeezes, I can keep up the pretence no longer.

"Just you."

I pull him to me, pressing my lips to his. He responds in an instant, deepening the kiss, plundering my mouth with his talented tongue. I open my eyes and look up, and for a second, the lights of the Eiffel Tower transform into shooting stars, falling all around us. But then my eyelids flutter shut and I'm lost in the sensations of Saul's lips on mine, his arms holding me tight, the weight of him as he presses me against the side of the bridge.

"I love you," I whisper when we come apart for air, the words escaping my lips before I can stop them.

Saul's hot breath rushes over my cheek as he chuckles. "I know."

Chapter Seventeen

BARUCHIEL

Adramelech set quite a pace, and Baruchiel struggled to keep up as he followed him down a pathway. Left to his own devices, he would never be able to navigate the complex maze, so Baruchiel had no choice but to trust that his new companion would not lead him astray. Their trajectory gradually became steeper and Baruchiel scurried forward a few paces, moving closer to Adramelech.

"Where are we going?"

Adramelech stared straight ahead as he barked, "Earth."

"But wh—?"

"Did you not hear what the messenger said? They've been sighted, so we're going to ferret them out. Then you can see first-hand what's going on. Hopefully, it will become clear to you why this is an internal matter, at which point you can fly back to the nest and assure your feathered fellows that there's no need for heavenly interference." He finally turned and looked at Baruchiel. "Got it?"

"I understand."

"Good. Ah, here we are at last." Adramelech veered to the right, and at the end of the path was a small doorway, barely large enough for them to pass through. "Make a quick exit, angel. The boss doesn't like these doorways open for too long, lest someone wander through by mistake. You wouldn't believe the nightmare of paperwork an incident like that causes!"

When Adramelech opened the door, Baruchiel squeezed through the gap. He blinked as he stepped into the earthly realm. It was night-time wherever they had emerged, but after the gloom of Hell's network, the lights from the mortals' buildings seemed bright and Baruchiel had to wait a moment for his eyes to adjust.

"Come on." Adramelech wasted no time. After securing the door, he strode towards a tall, illuminated structure a short distance away. "The scout told me this is where they were last seen. The information is recent. So, with luck, they won't have left yet." A grin spread across his face. "Ah yes, there they are, the fools. Saul deserves to be caught if he's going to be so careless."

Baruchiel followed the line of Adramelech's gaze and spotted two figures standing on a bridge. From this distance, they were mere shadows bathed in moonlight, arms around one another, looking out over the water. When Adramelech crept forward, Baruchiel followed suit. He had to admit, he was intrigued. He was not quite sure what he'd been expecting, but it certainly wasn't this. In fact, he wasn't even sure what 'this' was. Nothing he'd seen so far pointed to an internal matter, as Adramelech had claimed. But perhaps he was not yet getting the full picture; perhaps all would soon become clear.

As he moved closer, keeping low and quiet, Baruchiel saw the taller man lean in and kiss the other. When they broke apart once more, the shorter figure turned and his face was bathed in light. Baruchiel had to stifle a gasp. The young man could have been an angel. He certainly looked like one, with his blond curls and clear, bright eyes. If Baruchiel hadn't sensed the man's mortality, he would've believed himself to be in the presence of one of his brothers.

"Like seeing your reflection, eh?" Adramelech gave a low chuckle. "He's a pretty one, is he not, this Thomas Ives? I'm sure his appearance is half the reason the boss is so adamant that we can't let him get away. After all, it'd be almost like having one of you lot with us again. It's been a while since that last happened, so I imagine the boss wants to parade him 'round a bit, put on a show of strength, and—"

"*That* is Thomas Ives?"

Baruchiel was so thrown by this revelation that it took him a moment to register the other figure. When he did so, he shook his head, unable to accept what he was seeing. He looked again. But, no, he had not made a mistake.

"He's with a demon."

"Yep. Like I said, it's an internal matter. Saul here's the one who made the deal with the angel lookalike. Only things took an unexpected and far-from-welcome turn when the idiot suddenly up and imagined himself in love with the boy, or some other such nonsense. Love! Demons don't fall in love. We don't stand all doe-eyed on moonlit bridges, whispering sweet nothings into the ears of mortals." He waved aside the sceptical look Baruchiel cast his way. "Okay, we do...but we don't *mean* them. We only do it as part of the act, doing whatever it takes to get them to sign on the dotted line—always keeping within the rules, of course. But Saul here!" Adramelech paused to sneer. "He's gone off the deep end and no mistake, lost his marbles good and proper. Such a shame. He was once one of the best of us. He had a real artistic flair for dealmaking—a great favourite of the boss—and now look at him."

Baruchiel did look. He looked, and he smiled.

The demon was in his human form. Baruchiel could see the fiery darkness burning inside him, but no mortal would ever guess he was not one of them. It was a handsome exterior (Baruchiel could objectively tell that much) and he made a striking contrast with Thomas Ives—a meeting of dark shadows and pure light. The notion of a cursed demon and this angelic mortal being together should have felt vile, corrupt, and perverse. Yet there was something about them as a pair. Baruchiel couldn't quite put his finger on it, but they were...right.

He watched as Thomas turned back to Saul and pulled him into another kiss. This one was deeper than the last. More urgent. Passionate. And it wasn't simple lust. No, Baruchiel could see the bright, pulsing, golden glow of true love that surrounded them. And, to his surprise, it wasn't just flowing from Thomas. A light of equal brightness shone forth from Saul's body, enveloping Thomas in its radiance. It appeared that Adramelech was wrong: demons *were* capable of love. Adramelech couldn't see it, of course. Only angels could bear witness to the visible manifestation of true, selfless love.

Baruchiel thought back over his long existence, trying to recall a precedent for what was here before him, something that would explain what was going on. But he could think of none. As far as he knew, this was the first time a demon had fallen in love with a mortal. He was certain that whatever this was, it was something new and undocumented. He felt like a pioneer and thrilled at the thought of making his report to his superiors when he returned to Heaven. Except, he couldn't go home, could he? Not until he'd rescued Thomas Ives. As exciting and history-making as the current situation was, Baruchiel came down from his euphoria to realise that there was a much more pressing matter that needed his attention.

"So," Baruchiel began, clearing his throat and trying to keep his voice level, "what exactly are you planning on doing with them?"

A sinister smile lit Adramelech's face. "Both are coming down to Hell. Thomas Ives signed a contract and tried to break it. He belongs with us, along with all the other gullible mortal souls. As for Saul... He'll appear before the council. Officially, he'll get a fair trial, but between you and me, the boss is so pissed at him, he'll swiftly be found guilty of treason and sentenced accordingly. Some of my colleagues have set up a high-stakes pool regarding his punishment. Given my role in his capture and trial, I can't take part, but if I *could* place a bet, my money would be on either one hundred years imprisonment in one of the deepest Hell-Fire pits, if the boss is feeling generous, or else physical death and eternal torture for his soul."

Baruchiel contemplated his position. Technically, Adramelech was probably right to assert that the issue over the broken contract was an internal matter. Interference from Heaven in such a case would be unacceptable. Then again, this was more than just a broken contract. The situation was unique. And as such, surely the normal rules did not apply? His instructions had been to save Thomas Ives whatever the cost and Baruchiel could see only two potential reasons for that. On the one hand, it could be the boy's appearance. He did look like an angel. Was he of mixed angel–human parentage? It was a possibility, but it seemed unlikely *that* was the reason for the intervention since the nephilim were normally scorned—an embarrassment for Heaven best left unmentioned. On the other hand, maybe Heaven knew of this strange demon–human relationship and was keen to protect the boy on the basis of that. Either way, Baruchiel realised he'd have to make a choice, and soon. Should he stand by, allow Adramelech to drag the two men to Hell, and hope to free Thomas Ives later, or should he intercede at this juncture?

"Shit!"

Adramelech's exclamation drew Baruchiel from his contemplations and he looked up to see Thomas and Saul fleeing across the bridge, already nearing the opposite bank.

Adramelech leapt to his feet. "We've been made. Time to move in before we lose them."

Baruchiel bit his lip. There was no time to consult with Heaven first, no time to clarify his mission parameters. He would have to make the decision himself. As he acknowledged that fact, he realised that he had already made up his mind. He knew what he had to do.

Chapter Eighteen

SAUL

I know what you're thinking. You're rolling your eyes at that corny old line. Well, roll away. I may be a twenty-first-century demon, in touch with my yin and yang and all that jazz, but I'm still a bloke, and that 'L' word comes kinda hard. Sweet Tom has no problem with it, sure, but he's a sensitive, artistic type—it's easier for them. As for us demons... Look, can you keep a secret? Don't tell this to Tom. Don't hurt him. Do you promise? Thing is, I'd always been told that we couldn't love—demons, I mean—that it was impossible, that we weren't built that way. For all these years, I've believed it...and maybe I still do.

After all, this thing I'm feeling, what if it's not love? I don't know what else you'd call it, but it's gotta be a mistake. Right? A demon falling in love at all, let alone with a mortal—how could that happen? Whether you believe in fate or free will, someone somewhere has made a huge cock-up. That's what I can't help but think when I look into those breathtaking blue eyes of his. Every time I kiss him, every time I lie with him—I mean that in the Biblical sense; I don't always feel the need to be crude—I wonder, *Is this the last time? When the moment ends, will I blink and wake up to find this unnameable feeling gone?*

Don't misunderstand me; I'm not saying I *want* it gone. Hell knows, Tom's the best thing that's ever happened to me. I barely recognise myself since I've been with him. I actually *care* about things now—things other than personal gratification and my placing on the office leader board. I would go to the ends of the earth for that boy. I would attempt impossible deeds for his sake. Not that I've been horsewhipped or house-trained. I'm still the man, still wearing the pants, still in control. Don't think for one second that Tom has neutered me. I'm a kick-ass demon, top of the game when it comes to making deals, and nothing's going to change that. But I will concede that my priorities have taken a sharp turn.

I'm not ashamed to admit I was *pretty* self-obsessed prior to making that last deal. I make no excuses for that—all demons are the same. Why do you think we became demons in the first place? Now, though, I find myself thinking of Tom, putting his comfort and happiness before my own. When I reflect on what's ahead, on what will happen when...if...they catch us, I give precious little thought to my own fate. Him, on the other hand...the thought of what they would do to him down there...

I sense Tom's gaze. Then his hand is behind my neck and he's pulling me towards him. I go with the flow, happy to submit for a change, keen for anything to distract my thoughts from the dark place into which they had sunk a moment ago. His honeyed lips meet mine and I try not to crush him too tightly, not wanting him to taste the desperation in my kiss. A few seconds later, I no longer care.

I press him against the wall, farther and farther, until a slight backward motion tells me that he's almost half over it. I suppose it says something for how much confidence he has in me that he makes no panicked move forward, clearly trusting that I won't let him fall. And he's one hundred per cent right: I won't.

I move my arm behind his back for added support and then I claim those soft lips and that hot, wet tongue as my own. His body slots into mine so perfectly that I could almost believe that we were two halves of a whole, merging back into one. And I find I can no longer picture my life without him in it. Is this love? I honestly don't know the answer to that question any more now than I did a few minutes ago. Whatever it is, it's all-consuming and it burns as hot as the flames of Hell. No, that's not right. It's hotter. And cooler. At once, both violent and calming. Bursts of flame meeting a refreshing mountain spring. My darkness to his light.

Lost in the moment—and starting to envision some less-clothed moments we can have when we get back to the hotel—I almost miss it. I almost miss *him*. But then the faint waft of sulphur fills my nostrils, and I muster enough coherent thought to recognise there's a demon nearby. There's another scent too—something new—but it's the demon that draws my focus. He may just be passing through. He may not even have noticed us. Either way, we need to move. Right. Now.

I break the kiss so suddenly that Tom and I bump teeth. It's more irritating than truly painful, and I ignore the slight ache as I grab Tom's hand and drag him after me, back the way we came.

"Demon."

That one word is enough of an explanation to yank Tom out of his stupor, and a second later, he's no longer a dead weight but is running beside me. I can hear footsteps behind us. Guess that answers the question about whether or not this scumbag was here looking for us. Wonder whom the boss sent this time. Another delivery boy? An electrician? Perhaps a door-to-door salesman? I risk a glance over my shoulder.

Shit.

When Tom jerks, I realise I'm squeezing his hand too tightly, hurting him. I force the muscles in my arm to relax, but I also step up our pace another notch, and Tom matches me as we reach the end of the bridge and hurry across the road. It's a good thing traffic is light in the predawn hours because I don't even look for oncoming vehicles as we cross. All I can think of is putting as much distance between us and our pursuers as possible. This area is too open, too exposed. I need to get us back to Montmartre, where we can hide in the winding side streets with their shadowed doorways and, from there, double back to the hotel when the coast is clear.

Amidst the panic and the adrenaline rush of our flight, I feel a flicker of pride. To think that the boss has resorted to sending Adramelech! I know, I know. Now is hardly the time. Get away first and gloat later. Still, the boy and I are clearly bigger fish than I thought if they are sending the big guns after us now. Adramelech is a legend amongst demon-kind—a fallen sun god, a murderer of kings! For a while, way back when, he was the boss's right-hand man, until he dropped out of favour and others took his place at Satan's side. Even relegated down the ranks, he's a force to be reckoned with, and it's nice to learn that Tom and I are worth such immense effort and resources.

When we reach Monceau, I get my wits about me enough to notice something odd: a distinct lack of brimstone. I curtail my pace ever so slightly, not quite trusting my olfactory foramina. I take a good long sniff.

But the air is clean. Well, maybe not clean—I'm getting three-day-old garbage from the bins across the street (including the decaying remains of a chicken carcass), jizz from a condom discarded under the row of trees to our right (someone had a *very* good time tonight), and the usual pollution and body odours of a city centre (you learn to block them out after you've worked topside for a while)—but definitely no eau de Hell.

I glance behind, just to be certain, but the only person sharing the street with us is a homeless man asleep on a bench. Adramelech is nowhere in sight. Well, hooray...I guess. I'm thankful and all, yet our escape was altogether too easy for me to feel comfortable in our victory. Adramelech's been around for a long time—much longer than yours truly. He's a pro and we shouldn't have been able to outrun him that easily. Something else must have happened, and I don't like not knowing what that something was. No way am I crowing over this one until Tom and I have put a hundred miles or more between us and this city.

"Did we..." *Pant. Pant.* "...lose them?" *Pant. Pant.*

I slow us down to a fast walk and look over at Tom. He's a pretty fit guy, especially considering his nerd status, but we've run a fair way and I can see it's taken its toll. His curls are plastered to his head and a sheen of moisture coats his forehead. Hmm. Seeing him like this, all hot and bothered and gasping for breath the way he does after a steamy session between the sheets, is actually rather sexy. A bead of sweat trickles down towards his cheek, and I can't resist. I push him against the park fence, lean over, and lap up the nectar, tasting salt and...Tom.

"I'll take that as a yes, then."

He laughs and I find myself joining in. But then I remember who was chasing us and immediately sober.

"We seem to have lost them for now, but I don't want to take any chances. We're heading straight back to the hotel, packing, and getting the hell out of Dodge." I see his face fall and it makes my chest feel tight. "Sorry, sweet Tom, but it's no longer safe here."

He pulls a mask over his disappointment and nods. I take his hand, cast a final look left to right, to ensure the coast remains clear, and then we set off back to Pigalle.

Chapter Nineteen

Tom

Saul's packing is more frantic than usual. We've had some close calls before, but I've never seen him like this. I'd almost be tempted to say that he's afraid, except that this is Saul, and Saul's never afraid. He's the most courageous man...person...entity—What would be the politically correct term for a demon?—I've ever met. Even so...

I stand on the other side of the room and watch him. It's not a two-person job, and I'm not keen to get too close to him just now, not with the way he's flailing his arms around as he gathers our handful of possessions. I'd likely end up with an unintentional black eye or broken arm. The sound of the zipper cuts through the silence, and I catch his eye as he grabs the suitcase by its duct-taped plastic handle.

"Please, Saul, tell me what's wrong."

He offers me one of his widest grins, but the smile doesn't reach his eyes. "Nothing, my angel, just keen to get moving."

"No." I step forward and ease the case from his hand, setting it on the floor beside us. "Something's different this time. I can tell."

Saul sighs and runs his fingers through his hair. "The demon they sent... I got a look at him and I recognised him. He's a real player, Tom, not some two-a-penny minion. They're getting serious, and I'm not sure how much longer we can…" He frowns and lowers his gaze to the carpet.

I feel a tremor of fear. I've never seen Saul like this. He's always so sure, so cocky—the one who, without fail, pulls something out of the bag at the last moment, saving the day with a knowing, confident smile. But the expression currently in place on that handsome visage is one I've not seen grace his countenance before: despair mingled with resignation. I don't like it one bit. Luckily, I know one sure trick of my own, one trick that's guaranteed to bring him back to me.

"Kiss me."

Saul looks up. His brow remains furrowed, but I catch the gleam of hunger in his eyes and, as I'd hoped, it's enough to dispel the worst of that troubled expression.

"Kiss me," I say again, stepping closer, pressing my chest to his and tilting my head back.

Saul moans and his eyes flicker closed. "By Satan, Tom."

"Kiss me."

When he doesn't respond, I inch away far enough to slip my hands between us and then I start to undo the buttons on his shirt. He moves his arm, and for a moment, I think he's going to stop me, but then his hand falls back to his side and I continue to disrobe him. Once his shirt is open, I bend my head and run my tongue over each of his nipples in turn. A shudder passes through him; I feel the vibration against my lips, beneath my hands. I ease us towards the bed and this time he does offer a modicum of resistance, albeit only in words, not action.

"We need to leave, Tom. We do not have time for—"

Whatever he was going to say next is lost in a groan when I straddle him and brush my fingertips over the impressive tenting in his trousers. My own cock is already rock-hard and straining against the confines of my jeans.

This is a new feeling for me—being in charge this far into things. I love that Saul is possessive and dominant. I relish losing myself in him, cutting off my mind from everything bar our mutual pleasure for a few blissful minutes. Yet, it thrills me to see things from the other angle, to be above him, watching the effects of my touch, feeling that, in this moment, he'd do anything I ask. There's only one thing I want, though—to have my old Saul back—and I'm hoping this ploy will draw him from whatever shadows overpower him.

I reach down and unbuckle his belt, fumbling and hurried as I grapple with the clasp. It seems to take forever, but in reality it's the work of mere seconds to pop the button and pull down the zipper, and then I attain my prize. (Saul prefers to go commando most of the time and I'm thankful for one less layer to have to get through.)

I moisten my lips and lower my head, licking my way up his shaft from base to tip. He makes a glorious sound as I reach the top, and I quickly part my lips farther and take his full length into my mouth. *That* gets a reaction and I hum contentedly (and rather provocatively) as he bucks beneath me.

Within seconds he's gripping my upper arms, his thumbs digging into my flesh so hard that I'm certain there'll be bruises there by tomorrow—visible testimonies to his ardour that I will treasure until they fade away, or until he provides me with new ones. It's somewhat painful, yet pleasurable at the same time. The insistence of the touch makes me release him, and the moment my mouth leaves his cock, he flips us, rolling me onto my back as he climbs on top of me.

When I look up into his eyes, I'm relieved to see them burning with their old fire. My plan worked perfectly. Saul's a big talker, always jabbering away, but when it comes to things that really matter, he's as tight as a clam and actions get through to him more clearly than words. Tonight is a case in point.

He's already working the zipper of my jeans and I raise my hips as he scrambles to tug the tight denim down my legs, growling with frustration when it clings too persistently to my skin. My T-shirt follows—pulled inside out before being thrown to the floor as usual—and then my briefs, and I lie back and await instructions, happy to relinquish control to Saul once more.

He lifts my right leg and kisses his way from my ankle, along my calf and then down my inner thigh. I suck in a breath as he nears my groin, but before he gets there he pulls away and commences the same procedure on my left leg. This time when he stops at the top of my thigh I can't repress a whimper, and I hear him chuckle.

The mattress shifts as Saul leaves the bed, but then I hear a zipper, and a moment later, he returns. He runs a lubricated hand over my aching cock and I thrust into his palm. He allows me to do this twice before taking his hand away and shifting his fingers lower. The initial penetration tears a sigh from my lips, and I close my eyes and sink back into the pillows as he stretches me.

He takes his time and I begin to feel impatient. His fingers feel oh-so-nice, but I want more. I *need* more. I open my eyes and capture his gaze. From the way his mouth curves into a smile, my desperation must be pretty clear. He shifts, lifting first my right leg and then my left, hooking his arms under my knees. Then he pushes into me.

When I signed that contract the day I met Saul, I realised it would mean I'd never get to see Heaven. But then I spent that amazing night with him and I came to understand that I'd been wrong. I *have* been to Heaven. I go there every time Saul and I are joined. Heaven is the feeling of him inside me, filling me, claiming me as his own. It isn't angels with white wings playing on golden harps—it's so much more than that. It's belonging, it's peace, it's companionship... It's love.

Saul moves inside me in slow, deep thrusts. This is not the frenzy of our last encounter but an intense joining of bodies and souls. He presses down on me and leans in for a lingering kiss, exploring my mouth with his tongue, grazing my lips with his teeth. He releases one of my legs and moves his hand to my hair, sinking his fingers into my curls.

"My angel," he whispers.

He raises my other leg a little higher, altering the angle, and suddenly I'm seeing stars every time he buries himself within me. The feeling builds and builds until I can't hold back any longer, and I come, splattering both our chests with my release. Saul grips my hair tighter, his body tensing, and in the next moment, he pulses inside me, filling me with his seed, marking me as his once more.

He pulls out and rolls us both onto our sides, facing each other. He draws me closer and his hot breath beats against my forehead. "Thank you."

His voice is so low that I only just catch the words, and I shift back a little to look at him. His emerald eyes meet mine, and for half a second, I forget how to breathe.

"What for?" I ask when I regain the power of speech.

"For reminding me why we're doing this, why we have to keep running."

It's a simple statement, yet it makes my heart sing. He *does* still want to be with me. He does...care about me. I want to tell him that I love him, but I hold back, worried I'll ruin the moment. The 'L' word tends to make Saul nervous. I've never heard it pass his lips, and when I forget and say it in the heat of the moment, he usually resorts to humour or finds a way to change the subject. I don't mind. Not that I don't long to have him look at me and voice those three little words. But I know it's hard for him. And I know he does love me in his own way. Our relationship is unusual in the extreme, and I won't risk what we have by pushing him for something he's either not ready, or unable, to give.

He strokes his fingers down my arm and I push aside my reveries and return to the moment. His smile tells me that whatever worries he had have been allayed for now. He's looking at me as if he can't decide whether to laugh or ravish me again. The slight twitch of his cock against my thigh suggests the latter is a distinct possibility, and my own body responds at the thought.

Saul raises an eyebrow when he feels me harden against him and offers me one of his mock-shocked expressions. "So very eager tonight, my sweet Tom. Not even the threat of capture and eternity in a fiery pit in the depths of Hell is enough to diminish your ardour."

"We have to get going, don't we?"

Saul drops the act, his mouth levels out into a hard line, and he gives a single nod. "Yes, we need to make a move. I want to be out of here by the time the sun rises."

He pulls away from me and hurries to the bathroom. I hear the tap running, and he emerges a few seconds later, wiping himself off with a dampened towel. He tosses a second towel to me, and I catch it and clean myself as best I can without a full shower, before retrieving my clothes from the floor.

Barely five minutes later, we slide into the back seat of a taxi. The car whizzes us away in the direction of the station just as the first orange-pink tinge of dawn teases over the horizon.

Chapter Twenty

BARUCHIEL

Baruchiel had always been a diplomat and had never assaulted *anyone* before, let alone a demon. He wasn't even sure he had it in him—violence of any kind seemed so...rude—but he supposed he was about to find out. With no experience in combat, he had to rely on instinct to guide his actions. When he saw Adramelech make a move, he dove forward, stretching out his arms as far as he could reach. His fingers made contact with the demon's furry legs and he grabbed hold, toppling Adramelech, sending them both sprawling.

"What the hell do you think you're doing, you stupid angel?"

Adramelech clambered to his feet with a snarl, curling his hands into fists. He turned again towards the bridge, and Baruchiel sat up and scanned the right bank, breathing a sigh of relief when he saw no sign of Thomas Ives or his lover.

"Thanks to you, they got away!" Adramelech paced, gesturing wildly. "Now we'll have to start from scratch." He glared at Baruchiel. "But that's what you intended, wasn't it? This wasn't some bumbling-angel accident. You did this on purpose to prevent me from capturing the fugitives, didn't you? Is that why Heaven sent you here, angel scum?"

"No, Heaven did not instruct me to act in this way. I made the choice myself."

Adramelech barked out a dry laugh. "An angel making a decision on his own, without Daddy's guidance? Between you and Saul, it seems like the world as we know it is crumbling away." His mirth disappeared and his expression became grim. "But fly away now, little angel. I have work to do." With that, he stomped off.

"Adramelech. You cannot have Thomas Ives's soul."

Adramelech halted midstride and turned, a scowl plastered across his face, his eyes fiery. "Oh no? And what do *you* plan to do about it?"

It was a good question. And the truthful answer was that Baruchiel didn't have a clue. This was unprecedented and far removed from any of his previous assignments. He had no clue what path to follow. But he didn't plan on letting Adramelech know that.

"You will soon see. This is not over yet." That sounded good, did it not? Firm but vague.

Adramelech sneered. Then he departed, storming over the bridge with a clacking of hooves and in a flurry of ashen feathers.

Baruchiel watched until Adramelech passed out of sight. Then he sat on the ground. He wondered if he should have followed Adramelech. What if he picked up Thomas Ives's trail and dragged him to Hell before Baruchiel got wind of it? But no, he had delayed the fiend a good while and there had been no indication of the path the two men had taken by the time Adramelech crossed the bridge. They were safe. For now, anyway.

I have to find them first. Yes, that seemed the most sensible way forward. Going back to Hell was pointless—they'd stonewall him after what he'd just done—and returning to Heaven without having accomplished his mission would be equally futile. *What if I just go home to seek further instruction? I could take this matter to the archangels and ask for their counsel.* No, bad idea. For all he knew, he'd be thrown off the case, and there was something about this one that called to him. He could not forget the way the two of them had looked, standing together, lost in each other's embrace, the blaze of their mutual love one of the brightest he'd ever seen. He had to make sure they were okay, that Adramelech didn't catch up with them. Not to mention the fact that this was his first mission in untold years and he'd missed his work, missed the chance to make a difference, to do something good, to help mankind. He had to see it through. *That means my only option is to stay here and find them.* And then what? What would he do once he located them? *No point worrying about that now. I have to find them first. I can cross the next bridge when I come to it.*

Baruchiel got to his feet and brushed off his robes. He'd forgotten how dirty the mortal world could be, how cumbersome. He'd grown accustomed to spotless clouds and a pristine appearance, and it was disconcerting to be back in a place of dust and grime, of germs and pollution. He'd only been here five minutes, but already his white garments had taken on a distinctly grey tone.

Dawn had not yet kissed the distant horizon, but Baruchiel could feel the approaching transition from darkness to light. He took a step towards the bridge, only to change his mind. He'd never find them on foot. It had been centuries since he'd last visited this city and its pathways were no longer familiar to him. He wouldn't even know where to begin his search at ground level. No, he would have to take to the skies and hope for the best.

Closing his eyes, Baruchiel concentrated his energy and released the magic cloaking that surrounded him. As the spell fell away, his wide white wings unfolded from his back. He spread them out, stretching his tight muscles, and gave them an experimental flap. Being tied in place for so long, the feathers had clumped together, but now that air was free to move through them once more, they quickly fluttered back into place. Baruchiel had grown used to his wings being always unfettered during his time in Heaven and it had been strange and uncomfortable to pin them back.

He allowed himself a moment to revel in the feeling of the breeze ruffling his wings—it tickled but in a faintly pleasurable way—and then he cast a look about him. Seeing no one around, he bent his knees and pushed off, flapping his wings in forceful strokes to get airborne. Once his feet left the ground, he evened out, climbing higher and higher until he soared above the city streets. The tower to his left looked different from on high and he took a moment to circle it, marvelling at its geometrical metal frame. Then he was off, ready to begin the search.

He followed the widest path leading away from the bridge, looking for any sign of movement, any clue to guide him in the right direction. But the city was still in the lull between night and day. Barely a handful of creatures stirred and precious few of those were human. *How am I ever going to find them?* Then a thought struck him and he nearly laughed out loud at his stupidity. *Of course, I do not need to look for* them, *only their light.* The glow of love that surrounded the two of them was a beacon that would guide his way. *That* was what he needed to find.

He swooped over the city, back and forth, to and fro. *They would not have had time to quit this place yet. They must still be here. I just need to be patient. There!* Baruchiel descended closer to the tops of the buildings. In the street below, two figures exited a doorway and climbed into a moving metal box. It was definitely them. Even if he hadn't been able to recognise their faces from such a distance, there was no mistaking the luminous golden aura that engulfed them.

Baruchiel scanned the surrounding area, but he saw no sign of Adramelech, or any other demons for that matter. He curved his lips into a wide, joyful smile. *He had found them first.* Now he needed to follow them and keep them safe until he could decide what was to be done.

Chapter Twenty-One

SAUL

The corner of a carton of pickled gherkins is digging into my back. I can't see the writing on the carton, since it's nigh on pitch-black in here, but I know it contains pickled gherkins because I can smell the foul things. Even through the packaging, the stench is almost unbearable. I've never been a fan of pickled gherkins at the best of times, but after being boxed in by them for nearly nine hours, I'm pretty much ready to blast every pickled-gherkin manufacturer in the world into smithereens, sending them all to Hell where they belong. If I wasn't on the run, I'd do it. Don't think I wouldn't! But an act like that would draw too much attention, so I refrain and put up with the discomfort as best I can. Why don't I move? Well, I can't, can I? If I shift position by even a millimetre, I'll disturb Tom, and the sweet boy deserves a smidgen of uninterrupted slumber after the night we've had.

Tom's head is resting on my shoulder and his curls tickle my cheek as I angle my head a fraction to look down at him. Granted, I can't see much in this gloom, but when he exhales I feel the gentle puff of air as it wafts over my shirt, and I know every inch of his body so well I can picture it even without a light source to illuminate that delectable form. To have him at my side—that's worth the nightmare of this gherkin-infested ride.

I confess that I wasn't feeling all that great a few hours ago. For a brief moment there, I let the panic set in and I was no longer the cool cucumber you've come to know and love. The sight of Adramelech knocked me for six; I don't mind admitting it. I wasn't expecting things to escalate to that level quite so fast. In fact, with the gift of hindsight, I don't think I *ever* expected things to go this far when this cat-and-mouse game commenced. I didn't realise it until today, but a part of me assumed that this arrangement, this fleeing for our lives, would be temporary. I figured that if we avoided being caught long enough, the boss would eventually tire of the chase and give up, letting Tom and me get away scot-free. His sending Adramelech blows that theory clear out of the water. It seems the boss is *way* more serious about this than I thought. He means business...and that's bad news for me and my sweet boy.

Ah, Tom. He pulled me out of my stupor all right. He always knows just what to say—or do—as if he can read my mind. That naked interlude before we departed Paris was just what I needed to clear my head, shake out the cobwebs, and restore my focus. I'm not saying all my fears are now allayed. Far from it. However, I've succeeded in dispelling the dark mantle of despair. I've dusted off the drab cloak of disquiet. I've divested myself of— Well, you get the picture. I've never been a quitter, and I don't intend to start now.

Adramelech may be a pro, but he's a pro out of practice. For centuries he's been more bureaucrat than bloodhound, and it's been decades—maybe longer—since he was last topside. Plus, he's never come up against me before. Not to blow my own trumpet—well, maybe just a little—but I'm one skilled demon. Apart from being a real stunner in the looks department (no hooves or stupid feathers for me), an adept dealmaker (top of the league tables), and probably the greatest lover in the world (just ask Tom if you need confirmation on that one), I have one other valuable talent: I *know* this world. While Adramelech has been pushing papers across Hell's board tables, I've been mingling with the mortals, roaming their cities, keeping up with their ever-changing customs, and I've picked up a thing or two along the way.

Take our current location, for example. We could've left Paris by rental car, by plane, by boat, by train…but all would've left a trail. Even with our shiny false passports and assumed names—*Messieurs* John Constantine *et* Steve Rogers *à votre service*—it was too risky. So, with devilish cunning and the teeniest burst of magical camouflage, I snuck us into the back of this delivery truck. To be honest, I'm not even sure where it's heading, but it looked like the driver was gearing up for a long trip, and if *we* don't know where we're going, I can't believe anyone else will know, either.

Ghoulish gherkins aside, this was a real smart move, if I do say so myself. Hopefully, wherever we end up, we'll last longer than a day before being discovered this time. It was a grave error of judgment to get all sentimental and take Tom out of the hotel with me—a mistake I will *not* be making again. And yet, for those few minutes on that stupid, moonlit bridge, he was blissfully happy. I could see it in his smile, in his eyes. Hell, I could feel his joy pulsing through his fingertips when he pulled me in for a kiss. I could taste the sheer contentment on his lips. And the Devil knows, my single goal in life these days, my greatest wish—aside from keeping one step ahead of the boss and his lackeys—is to make my Tom happy.

Bah, listen to me! The others down below would never let me hear the end of it if they witnessed me carrying on like some sappy, lovesick mortal fool. Tom is already happy. He must be—he has me, after all, and what more could anyone, man or woman, mortal or demon, want? Look, I can sense you rolling your eyes, making out you're not convinced, but who're you to talk? *You* keep following me around like a stray dog. We both know *you* can't get enough of little old *moi*, always yapping at my heels, desperate for my attention. Nah, I'm not complaining. You can stay. But quit it with the judgment. Okay?

My shoulder's starting to ache now and I long to stretch. Even so, I refuse to budge. Nothing in Heaven or Hell will induce me to disturb Tom's rest. Nothing!

I guess I should have thought to add 'Earth' to my declaration because, mere seconds after my firm avowal, we hit a bump in the road and I'm forced to extend my hand to steady myself against another pile of cartons. The movement shakes Tom awake; I feel him stir against me.

"Saul? Where are we?"

I grin. "I have absolutely no idea!"

Tom won't be able to see my smile, but I'm sure he'll hear it in my voice. I want him to feel relaxed, safe. I don't want to give him any cause for worry. Not until it becomes necessary. And it's not necessary at present, is it? This plan of mine is a good one, I'm certain of it, and surely it will take them a while to pick up our trail again, unless we get *very* unlucky and run into a sycophantic demon dogsbody the second we exit the vehicle. No, for the moment at least, we can rest secure. And nothing says 'secure' like a little humour.

"Exciting, isn't it, Tom? We're charting courses to lands unknown, exploring new frontiers, going where no demon–human couple on the run has ever gone before.

You're the Spock to my Kirk, the Robin to my Batman."—
I like to throw a few comic-book references into our
conversations whenever I can, knowing it pleases him—
"It's like I'm the Lone Ranger and you're my Tonto."

Tom laughs. "I suppose I can live with Tonto. For a
moment there, I was worried you were going to cast me
as Silver."

Oh, now *that's* an interesting idea. All my remaining
cares and worries melt away as my furiously fertile
imagination conjures a number of delightful scenarios.
The stirring scenes running through my mind provoke a
stirring of a more physical kind. I've wondered a few
times lately if my cock even belongs to me anymore. I
have the distinct impression it renounced my lordship
and transferred its allegiance to Tom that very first night.
Lucky for me, my sweet Tom is a benevolent ruler, always
keen to see to his subjects'...needs. Speaking of which...

"You as Silver? Never, sweet boy." I lower my voice to
a seductive whisper. "Unless, of course, you *want* me to
ride you."

I run my hand up his leg to his groin, and damn if he
isn't already half-hard. Ah, me and my silver tongue.
Better add that to my list of killer skills.

"But we haven't... I mean...we don't usually...do
things...that way."

I may not be able to see the blush, but I can hear it in
his voice and, oh, it's delectable. He blushed all the time
that day we first met, and for most of the initial week we
spent together, but he's less easily shocked these days,
and those marvellous red-pink flushes have become a
rare occurrence. Bringing one forth once more gives me
a great deal of pleasure, and I lift my free hand to cup his
face. The heat emanating from his cheek sends shivers
down my spine. The heat warming my other palm from a
lower, and by now rock-hard, source isn't half bad, either.

"One should always try new things, Tom," I say, rubbing back and forth over that rigid bulge, my touch light, teasing. "Just because we haven't done something yet, doesn't mean it's off the table...or the bed." I lean in and ghost my lips over his, eliciting a desperate groan. "Would that please you, my angel? Do you like the idea of a little role-swapping? Imagine it, Tom! You would lie back amidst the pillows, looking up at me, your eyes never leaving mine as I lower myself onto you. Slowly. One...inch...at...a...time. I would take you inside me, all of you, right to the hilt, gripping you oh-so-tightly. And then? Why, then I would ride you so hard and so fast you'd see stars, and the only word you'd be able to remember by the time I'm done would be my name. Would you like that, my sweet Tom?"

Tom convulses and the scent of cum fills the air. I decide to take that as a yes.

I release him and give him a moment to recover. I'm still hard, but that can wait. As much as the idea of desecrating this holy gherkin shrine pleases me—not to mention the anticipation of following through on the suggestion I just made to Tom—I don't want to be caught *in flagrante delicto* when we reach our destination. Not from any sudden modesty or sense of public decency, you understand, but in case there's a demon waiting for us at the other end. When this truck stops, I want to be ready to move.

"God, Saul!"

Ah, Tom's rejoined me. Out of the world of sexual bliss and back into the realm of the coherent comes the sweet angel.

"Wrong camp, dear boy, but I'm not averse to a little worship, if you wish to bestow it."

Tom's breathing is still heavy, and he reaches for my hand, which I willingly relinquish to his care.

"I'm all… I need to get changed."

Hmm. *That* seems a crying shame. I rather like smelling his release on the air, and the thought of his current dishevelled state is alluring. No, I don't think any cleaning up should be on the cards just yet.

"Stay like that, Tom. Just for a while. To please me?" I run my hand through his curls and grab ahold, pulling him in for a kiss.

At that moment, the truck splutters to a halt, and I hear the squeak of the handbrake, followed by the slam of the driver's door. At first, I wonder if it's merely another pit stop, but, no, there comes a series of *clunks* and the screech of metal as the doors at the back open. Ladies and gentlemen, we have arrived at our destination. I reluctantly let go of Tom and use the cursed gherkin cartons to pull myself to my feet. For better or worse, it's time to see where we've ended up.

Chapter Twenty-Two

TOM

The main thing on my mind at present is a strong desire for a shower. The inside of my briefs has gone from sticky to crusty and it's uncomfortable. Thanks to the thick denim of my jeans, you can't see a telltale stain, but judging by some of the odd looks passersby are casting my way, I must be walking funny. Or maybe I just look like I spent the last nine hours sleeping on the floor in the back of a truck—I'm probably a complete wreck.

Saul has been grinning from ear to ear ever since we arrived. That may be in part due to our spectacular escape—not a demon in sight as we emerged from the truck and made our way to the city centre—but I suspect my soiled state has some part to play in his happy mood. Aside from the slight discomfort, I don't mind. If he's happy, I'm happy. Isn't that what they say? It's a tad clichéd, I fear, but in this case, it happens to be true. You know, if we weren't so busy being on the run, I think Saul would find us some amazing apartment, all silks and leathers, and would have us stay in a luxurious king-sized bed twenty-four seven. He'd delight in making me come over and over and over again until I'm too exhausted to continue. It's a pretty attractive dream from my side of the equation, too, but one I doubt we'll be able to experience in this lifetime. Not unless Hell suddenly changes its policy on deal-breakers.

Talking of experiences, our current location is another new one for me: Prague, the Golden City. Our stowing-away got us as far as the outskirts, and we made our way into the city by bus. There was some issue over tickets when we boarded, but whatever Saul whispered to the driver worked because we were allowed to take our seats. Right now, we're mingling with the tourists in the Old Town Square while Saul picks out a place for us to call home for the next few days.

I stare about me, goggle-eyed and alert. Until I met Saul, I'd never left England, not even to go as far as Wales. I'd acquired the passport that sits in the desk drawer in my flat in preparation for a long-planned, and highly anticipated, trip to San Diego Comic Con next year. Now I've been in two different countries in the space of twenty-four hours.

Prague beckons me, foreign and mysterious, and I wish the circumstances of our visit were different so that Saul and I could explore its winding streets together. I try to picture what it would be like to stroll down these laneways hand in hand, no need to rush, no need to look over our shoulders every few seconds. We'd stop and take photos: of the scenery, of each other. I imagine a myriad of selfies with heads and chins cut off as we try to get both us and the historic landmark before which we'd no doubt be standing into the frame. It's another beautiful dream, but once again, I fear it's one we'll never see become reality.

The hour strikes and the tourists pause to ooh and ahh beneath the astronomical clock as it goes through its decorative motions. I have to admit, it *is* rather impressive, and I slow to a halt and join them, gaping up at the revolving figurines. Saul doesn't say anything, but I can sense his burst of nervous impatience as he hovers by my shoulder. So, a moment later, I leave the others to tick the clock off their Prague to-do lists and hurry after him as he cuts down a side street.

A sign to my left catches my eye and I stop again without meaning to, taken by surprise. Having acknowledged that I haven't gone mad, that the sign *does* say what I think it says, I try to move on before Saul notices my pause. I know I've failed in this endeavour when I hear him chuckle.

"Sex Machine Museum, eh?" His breath tickles my ear. "Now, why would a sweet angel like you be interested in a place like that? Is there something in there you desire, Tom?" He takes a step closer, pressing in behind me. "Something you need, perhaps?" A pause, and a change in tone. "Am I no longer enough to keep you satisfied?"

I feel a tightening in my chest. "No, no, Saul, of course you're en—" When I turn, I catch the glint in his eye and realise he's teasing me. I give him a light punch in the arm and shake my head. "Bastard."

"You wouldn't have me any other way. Come on, I know a nice little place nearby. Let's see if they have a room available."

FORTY MINUTES LATER I'm towelling myself off, clean and refreshed and feeling ready to face the world again. I sort through my T-shirts, looking for one in reasonable shape, but they're all equally crumpled, so I grab the first that comes to hand—Loki sitting on a throne—and tug it over my head. I find a fairly fresh pair of briefs and pull those on next. The jeans will definitely need washing soon, but I decide they're still wearable for now and yank them on too.

I shift the suitcase to the floor and flop onto the bed. My hair is damp from the shower and the occasional bead of moisture tickles its way down my neck, seeping into the collar of my T-shirt. I grab the remote control from the bedside table and turn on the television. I flick through the handful of channels provided, but they're all in Czech and I can't make out a single word, so I give up.

A rummage through the drawers in the bedside table reveals a copy of the Gideon Bible. It's in English and looks brand-spanking-new, barely out of its wrapper, but I set it back in its recess and close the drawer. I've already sold my soul to the devil; I think it's a tad late for me to be seeking religious guidance or spiritual solace. I pick up the hotel's information folder instead and flick through it. Checkout is at the usual two p.m.; breakfast will be served from seven until nine each morning; room service is available (at a premium); I must dial one-one-two to contact the emergency services; and the exits are here, here, and here. I notice they have a laundry service, and I make a mental note to mention it to Saul. If we're staying for a few days, it would be good to give my clothes a quick freshen up.

The pages farther back in the folder list some of the city's top attractions and options for day trips. I linger over them for a moment or two, picking out the sights I'd like to see. It's a futile exercise since I know I won't be setting foot outside this hotel room for the duration of our stay—no way will Saul sanction it after Paris—but the task helps to pass a few tedious minutes nonetheless. God, what I wouldn't give for a comic book right now! I'd offer my soul, but that ship has already sailed, and Saul would be upset if he knew such a thought had even crossed my mind. If only Saul were here. Then I'd have either sex or conversation to keep me occupied. As it is, a heavy cloud of ennui settles over me.

Saul went out just before my shower. He wanted to run a quick perimeter check to make sure there was no demonic activity in our general locale, and I guess that's wise. But his absence leaves me exposed. Not to demons. Rather, to my thoughts—and those do plague me like the devil when Saul isn't here to cast them aside with his presence.

The truth is that I'm conflicted; I have been for a while now. I love Saul. That will always be true, even if I never find out the extent of his feelings for me. I mean, it's clearly more than just physical. He could have anyone he desired—man or woman—and yet he risked everything to be with me. I know he cares about me. But it's that very care that has led to the predicament in which we now find ourselves. He wants to protect me, and so far I've let him. God knows I want to be with him. I don't want to be dragged down to Hell and never see him again. Yet, more and more lately, I've asked myself, *What about Saul?*

He may be the one who destroyed the contract, but in many ways, this is *my* flight. *I'm* the one trying to get out of a deal. They're only pursuing Saul because he's on the run with me. At times like this, when I'm alone, I wonder if I shouldn't surrender to the other demons on the condition that they absolve Saul of any blame. Would it even work? Would they let him go after everything he's done for me? I don't know. However, the idea will not leave me be.

The sound of knocking captures my attention, shaking me back to reality, and I look towards the door. It's only when the sound comes again that I realise I've turned my head in the wrong direction. The knocking isn't coming from the hallway. It's coming from the other side of the window...and we're on the second floor.

Chapter Twenty-Three

BARUCHIEL

Baruchiel was tired. And angels didn't tire easily. It had been a simple thing to follow Thomas and Saul as they crept into the back of the moving rectangular box and made their way out of the city. He'd flown above them, enjoying the freedom and the sense of adventure—something that had long since ceased to exist in his day-to-day life. He'd decided to approach them the next time they stopped. He would take them with him when he returned to Heaven, and that would keep Thomas Ives and his lover safe until Baruchiel could consult with the others and find out how to proceed. It had seemed an excellent plan. Only, they didn't stop.

By the time the fugitives emerged, several long hours later, Baruchiel's wings were killing him. He hadn't dared to pause for a breather lest he lose sight of his charge, and he was paying for that now. Every flap of his wings, every ruffle of his feathers, was pure agony. Had someone offered him the chance in that moment, he thought he'd gladly have given up his wings forever in exchange for a soft bed of cloud.

When Thomas and Saul entered the hotel, Baruchiel waited. He held back, partly to catch his breath and partly to be certain no demons were nearby before he made his move. A few minutes later, Saul emerged alone and set off down the street. To the humans, it would look like he was out for a casual stroll, but Baruchiel could sense the alertness in his eyes. For an instant, Saul peered in Baruchiel's direction, a puzzled expression passing over his face, but Baruchiel reinforced the shield that hid his angelic aspects from those around him, and in the next breath, Saul turned away and continued his patrol.

Baruchiel considered his options. Should he await Saul's return or approach Thomas while he was alone? On reflection, the latter seemed the better option. As a demon, Saul would have...certain views about angels and might be wary of going up to Heaven. If Baruchiel could convince Thomas first, the mortal would help to persuade his lover and Baruchiel's job would be simpler.

The next question was how to approach. He could enter the building and seek out their room from within, or he could force his wings through one more burst of flight and try the windows. Despite the ache in his limbs, the external approach seemed the better path to follow. Knocking on the door when Thomas was likely expecting a demon to attack at any moment could only lead to confusion and potential injury. Through the window, it would be clear to the mortal that Baruchiel was an angel, and hopefully things could proceed more smoothly.

He rose, wincing against the pain, and made his way from window to window. It didn't take long before he was drawn to a golden glow emanating from behind closed curtains. It had to be Thomas's room. He hovered in front of the pane of glass and rapped three times. When there was no response, he tried again, a little louder.

The second attempt produced a response and Baruchiel lowered the barrier masking his presence as the curtains were tweaked cautiously aside. He offered a broad smile that he hoped would allay any immediate fears, and it seemed to work because Thomas flung the curtains wide.

Baruchiel tapped again on the glass and gestured for Thomas to open the window. Thomas took a step back instead, his gaze assessing, unsure. Baruchiel pondered for a moment. Then he waved a hand towards his wings, giving them an extra flap for good measure, placed his palms together as if in prayer, and finally pointed to Heaven.

The mime show had the desired effect. Thomas approached the window and fumbled at the catch. When the glass opened outward, Baruchiel edged to the side, out of its path.

"Greetings, Thomas Ives. My name is Baruchiel."

"Um...hi." Thomas bit his lower lip and ran his fingers through the damp curls that clung to the side of his head.

He seemed confused, which Baruchiel found understandable, given the circumstances. After all, there was an angel flying around outside his hotel-room window, and that angel's appearance all but matched his own. It was possible—probable, in fact—that Thomas believed this to be a dream or a hallucination. That was par for the course. It had taken Gabriel several hours to convince Mary all those years ago. She'd required him to perform a vast number of party tricks before she'd even deigned to talk with him, let alone contemplated allowing...anything else. Baruchiel hoped Thomas's wealth of experience with demons would make him more credulous, since time was very much of the essence in this case.

"You are not imagining this, Thomas, nor do you need to fear me. I am an angel, sent here to save your soul from Hell."

"You're here to help us? Can you really help us?"

Well, it hadn't taken Thomas long at all to accept who—and what—Baruchiel was. That certainly made things easier. The hopeful tremor in Thomas's voice was to be expected, but what Baruchiel found more interesting was his choice of pronoun: not 'me' but 'us'. Baruchiel did not doubt that, were he to say that he was only here to help Thomas and not the demon, too, Thomas would refuse all aid. It was a realization that filled Baruchiel with both euphoria and a deep foreboding. It gladdened his heart to see such love, such devotion, yet he wondered how much he could promise. His personal wish would be to save them both— regardless of what Saul was, what he represented, and what he had done in the past—but his official instructions had listed only Thomas. Would Heaven support him if he said he would save Saul as well, or would he have to go back on his word?

"I am certainly going to try." There, that seemed a good compromise—a promise that didn't commit him either way. "The demons have not found you here yet, but they will. I believe it best if you both accompany me to Heaven. We can keep you safe there while we see about cancelling Hell's claim on you."

"Why do you look like me?"

Ah, there it was: the question Baruchiel had anticipated would crop up at some point. The one to which he did not have a clear answer.

"I believe it would be more correct to say that *you* look like *us*."

"All angels look the same?"

"Not in every tiny detail, but in general, yes. We all have roughly the same hair, the same eyes, the same nose... As to why you share our appearance, I cannot say for certain. It may be you are a nephilim, or descended from one—the product of a human–angel coupling. Others in Heaven may have more answers in that regard. But we need to get there first."

Baruchiel stretched his arm through the window, reaching towards Thomas, intending to offer him a reassuring touch. The conversation had been going well, progressing at an excellent pace, and Baruchiel was feeling more and more confident about his plan. But his well-meant action caused an immediate and dramatic shift in the mood.

Thomas scurried backward, retreating from the window until he collided with the edge of the bed. "Please don't take me away. I don't want to go anywhere without Saul."

"No, no. I did not mean to suggest any such thing."

Baruchiel raised his hands, palms outward. He was so intent on alleviating Thomas's fears, he failed to notice when the door to the room swung open. He remained unaware they were no longer alone until a voice rang out, deep and dripping with menace.

"I don't know who in Hell you think you are, or what new trick the boss is trying to pull, but you keep your goddamn hands off him!"

Baruchiel knew he needed to say something to defuse the situation, but he was caught off guard and the words died on the tip of his tongue. By the time he'd gathered his wits enough to form a comprehensible response, it was already too late.

The ball of fire smashed into his chest, blasting Baruchiel back from the window. Between the impact of the flames and his shock at the dramatic turn events had taken, Baruchiel was too stunned to think clearly. His wings failed him and he spiralled out of control, tumbling towards the ground.

Chapter Twenty-Four

SAUL

It's been a few years since I was last in Prague, but the city hasn't changed much. Well, there is now a plethora of tacky souvenir shops, their signs helpfully translated from Czech to English to entice the ever-growing numbers of Western tourists, and I can see a marked increase in drunken groups of British visitors. Yes, a few are already drunk, even at this time of day, and if I weren't currently on an unscheduled leave of absence, I'd be eyeing up a few of them as potential marks and no mistake! They're here to make the most of cheap alcohol as they celebrate hens' nights and bucks' parties. They come to this city of absinthe and chase the elusive Green Fairy in an attempt to forget they'll soon be chaining themselves to another. Not irrevocably, perhaps, but one thing is certain: they won't be making any more such trips once their other half's previously bare finger is securely 'ringed'. Not unless they can persuade a friend to tie the knot, to precipitate another weekend away.

But for all that, the old part of the city remains otherwise intact, and if it's lost a little of its Eastern-bloc mystery over the last couple of decades, it still has charm and a certain magic. Not quite the level of magic it had in centuries past, when demons were a common sight along the cobbled streets and eager, Faustian alchemists provided a ready supply of souls ripe for the plucking, but a certain *je ne sais quoi* remains all the same. Perhaps it's the lingering memory of the olden days that leaves its mark on the modern city.

I meander the streets of this still-fair capital, allowing the general flow of pedestrian traffic to sweep me along until we reach the Charles Bridge. The angle of the sun as it begins its late-afternoon descent creates long shadows from the many statues lining the bridge's walls, and I have to raise my hand to shield my eyes as I look out over the steadily coursing waters of the Vltava. I pretend to stare up at the castle across the river as I scan the area for any signs of demonic activity. I sense something, but the scent is old and fading fast. There's nothing to indicate any demons are in the vicinity now and I breathe a sigh of relief.

Having ascertained there's no immediate threat, I relax my guard a little and lean back against the wall, watching the people milling in the square. The tourists are easy to spot, all goggle-eyed as they take in the city sights, wandering in front of oncoming cars and trams, obstructing the laneways as they stop and gape. The locals are the ones dashing to and fro, casting withering looks at the oblivious tourists who block their way.

Ending up here was lucky. It gives us a breather. It allows us to regroup after a close call. The closest yet, and the most deadly, considering who now dogs our heels. It was *too* close this time; however, I don't know what more we can do. If I thought they'd accept me and leave Tom be, I'd have given myself up already, taken one for the team, accepted my fate. More altruistic a response than you'd have expected from me, I'm sure. Goes to show how much a relationship can change a man. And I *have* changed in some ways, it's true, but I'm still no fool. Even if the boss's minions scout's-honour-promised me Tom's safety in return for my surrender, I'd never be able to trust them to keep their word. Believe it or not, demons lie. Hey, don't go getting all judgmental on me; it's in our nature. You might even say that it's part of our job description.

No, they'll never let Tom go, not now Adramelech's involved. Our only option is to keep running for as long as we can, and as far as we can. I reckon we'll be all right to hole up here for a few days, since our entry was unexpected and it's unlikely we've picked up a tail. But where to next? Taking a chance on that truck worked out exceedingly well this time, but there's no guarantee that will always be the case. The mode of transport is a good one—and it will keep them all guessing, leaving no paper trail of tickets and bookings—but not knowing where we'll end up has a downside.

We lucked out with Prague since demons all but gave up on it as suitable soul-hunting ground when the Wall came down. I doubt that will last—the new wave of booze parties will lure my fellows back soon enough—but for now it's something of a safe haven. What if we'd wound up somewhere else though? What if we'd found ourselves stranded in one of the current vacation hotspots for the eighteen-to-thirty age bracket? The mere contemplation of such an occurrence sends shivers down my spine.

No, it's not the drunken rowdiness I'm trying to avoid, nor the excessive nudity. Come on, surely you know me well enough by now to know that those things are likely to attract rather than repel me. And *there's* the problem in a nutshell. Anywhere you find young people with loose morals, pissed and drugged out of their minds, you'll find an equally large population of demons. We'd be swamped the second we exited the truck. Such places are prime hunting ground for those of us who dwell below. Those crazy kids are controlled by their egos. It's all "me, me, me"—and they will sign *anything*.

I personally find the whole scene rather distasteful in terms of making deals. I mean, there's hardly any skill, any finesse, in getting a twenty-year-old girl, high on a cocktail of who-knows-what, to sign a contract in exchange for a quick fuck. Some will even sign in exchange for another drink! And with the amount of flesh they're usually displaying by then, they'd easily get someone to buy them a drink without having to pay for it with their soul. But they're too far gone by that stage to realise that simple truth, and it's all too easy for my colleagues to swoop in. I know some demons who work exclusively in the clubbing resorts these days. I have more pride in my work than that. I only haunt the Mediterranean bars if I'm *desperately* short on my quota for the month. When you have my skill, you can be top dog without resorting to lowbrow tactics. I think it would be fair to say that I'm one of the last remaining artists amongst my kind. It takes a demon of innate talent and subtlety to secure a signee of my Tom's calibre, and I don't mind saying so myself. I know you agree with me, even if you think yourself too morally superior to speak the words aloud.

Thoughts of Tom draw me out of my internal monologue and refocus my mind. After conducting a final sweep of the square—it remains demon-free—I decide it's time to make my way back to the hotel. The idea of staying in that red-and-gold room with him for an uninterrupted (save for room-service meals) forty-eight hours of mind-blowing sexual escapades is one that grows all the more appealing with every step I take.

Planning our next move can wait for a couple of days—a concept I agree with all the more wholeheartedly when I think back to our recent conversation in the back of the truck. It could be fun to try something new between the sheets. And it won't require me to relinquish control *completely*. I'll still be on top—both literally and figuratively—only rather than ploughing his awesome arse, I'll be fucking myself on his captivating cock. Mmm. The thought of it is enough to make me salivate.

I enter the hotel lobby and make my way to the compact but pristine lift. I punch the button for the second floor and hum to myself as the car ascends—*Animal* by Neon Trees. And, yes, in case you're wondering, I *do* want some more, and I anticipate getting it within the next two minutes. If this stupid contraption will just move faster.

When we finally attain the desired *poschodí*, I hasten out of the lift and speed down the corridor in the direction of our room, already pulling the key from my pocket—a good old-fashioned key this time instead of those stupid electronic cards.

I know something is wrong the moment I reach the door. That unfamiliar presence I sensed back in Paris is here. It's here—and it's in there with my sweet Tom. My emotions yo-yo. For an instant, I'm honest-to-Satan not sure whether I'm afraid or angry—probably a bit of both, I guess. Anger finally wins out and I slot the key into the lock, fling open the door, and stride into the room. I see Tom backing away from a figure at the window and I don't wait a second longer.

"I don't know who in Hell you think you are, or what new trick the boss is trying to pull, but you keep your goddamn hands off him!"

Something about the figure is off, unexpected, unusual, but I can't quite put my finger on what, and I don't have time to stand around and ponder now—I have to act. I pull up a nice big burst of Hell-Fire from one of the pits down below, gather the flames into a ball in the palm of my hand, and then hurl the missile with all my might. It's a good throw by anyone's standard, a clean hit to the chest that sends my adversary flailing backward. By my reckoning, the score is Saul: 1; Hell: 0.

A second later, the figure is plummeting and I'm reaching for Tom. There's no time to pack, no time to gather any of our possessions. New clothes are easily acquired; Tom is irreplaceable. I latch on to his arm and yank him from the room. I hear him speaking, but the words don't make it from my ears to my brain. All I know is that we're in danger and have to flee the scene. For all intents and purposes, it's a case of "exit, pursued by bear".

For some unfathomable reason, Tom's digging in his heels and I have to rely on my superior strength to drag him down the corridor to the emergency exit. It's not until we're in the stairwell, with the door firmly closed behind us, that my mind catches up with the rest of me and I comprehend what he's saying.

"Saul, you just set fire to an angel!"

An angel? A fricking angel? No! Yes? Really? A real-life angel? That does explain the odd scent. In all my years, I've never met an angel face-to-face before. I know they're up there in the clouds, but they rarely descend to earth anymore, so our paths don't often cross. Heaven and Hell prefer to keep to their own, and to my knowledge, no one's ever suggested an interoffice mixer.

Oh well, a rare new experience for me—my first-ever angel! And I shot the guy in the chest. Oops. Oh, don't shake your head like that. How was I supposed to know? When I see a threat to Tom, I react. Sue me.

I look over at Tom. His face is lined with concern, his baby blues wide, his lips parted. I release his arm and he rubs at it with his other hand. Double oops—looks like I was gripping a tad too hard during our sort-of escape.

"Baruchiel said he was here to help us. We need to find out if he's okay."

The day isn't getting any better. Not only did I toast an angel, it was apparently an angel offering aid. Angels are not usually known for providing assistance to demons—but if other demons react the way I just did, that's not all that surprising. Not that I in any way assume this heavenly visitation is for yours truly. If that angel's here to help anyone it will be my sweet Tom. Either way, it seems I've made something of a faux pas.

Part of me still thinks we should run for it. Even if this Baruchiel is on our side—and remains willing to help after my impromptu attack—a fireball like that, followed by an angel falling from the skies, is likely to have attracted attention. A few gawking mortals I can handle, but if it drew anyone else...

I cast another glance at Tom and realise that I don't have much of a choice. He's not going to walk away from this, not without ascertaining if his new best friend— Okay, I confess, I may have felt the *teeniest* stab of jealousy then—is still alive and kicking. It looks like we're going out into the street.

"Okay," I say, setting off down the stairs. "We'll see if he's still there."

I've gotta say, I have a *really* bad feeling about this. Something tells me I'm going to come to regret not knocking Tom unconscious, slinging him over my shoulder, and making off with him, caveman-like, while the coast is clear. I could've beat my breast as I went, to make the image complete. But what can I do? I guess maybe I *have* been a little horsewhipped after all. But only a little, mind you. I prefer to see it as indulging him. Either way, I suppose you could argue that I'm a besotted fool with a good ninety percent of my brain function located in my trousers. I only hope the remaining ten percent is not about to fail me.

Chapter Twenty-Five

Tom

When we reach the ground floor, Saul gestures for me to hold back as he gingerly opens the fire-escape door. He glances left to right and then waves me forward. I keep close behind him as we make our way down the narrow alleyway. I'm dancing from foot to foot, gripping the hem of my T-shirt, which soaks up the sweat from my palms. Saul is moving so slowly that I wonder if we'll ever make it to the main street. I know he's just being cautious, but for all we know, Baruchiel is lying in a heap of shattered bones on the pavement. He may need medical assistance. And we are taking far too long to reach him.

I can't help but feel responsible for any injuries he's sustained. If I hadn't reacted so impulsively, getting worked up over a simple miscommunication, Saul would've entered the room to a very different scene and probably wouldn't have acted the way *he* did. I say 'probably' because I know zilch about angel–demon relations. It could well be they attack each other on sight as a matter of principle—like fans from rival football clubs after a match. But the impression I got from Saul's words, and his attitude as he yanked me out of the room, was that he'd acted solely in defence of me, which fills me with all manner of warm, fuzzy feelings...but which also led to an angel taking a fireball in the chest. I now understand how the love interest of superheroes must feel, their lives a constant rotation of kidnapping and rescue, kidnapping and rescue, leaving a slew of incapacitated villains and dead henchmen in their wake.

We finally reach the end of the alley and I peer around Saul's shoulder to look into the street beyond. Well, the good news is that Baruchiel's still with us, or at least his body is. The bad news? He's flat on his back on the ground with a sizeable crowd gathered around him. Saul swears under his breath and I echo the sentiment. He curses again, even louder and more vehemently this time, when I scoot around him and dash towards the fallen angel.

As I approach, I hear the mutterings of the crowd. It's a wild mix of different languages, some of which I recognise, others unfamiliar to my untrained ear, but I'm able to pick out enough English words to get a reasonable grasp on the impression the bystanders have formed. The general consensus appears to be that this was some kind of acrobatic act—advertising a forthcoming circus performance no less—gone wrong. They think the wings are part of his costume, which I guess is a good thing. At least no one seems to be mentioning either miracles or heavenly judgment...so far.

I sense Saul behind me as I ease my way through the crowd. He speaks loudly: a brief couple of sentences, repeated in several different languages. When he finally reaches English, I hear him tell the crowd that we're friends of the injured performer and will look after him, if they would be so kind as to step back and give the guy room to breathe.

The sea of bodies parts and I drop to my knees at Baruchiel's side. His chest is rising and falling at a steady pace, but his eyes are closed, and as I watch, a thin trickle of blood runs from the corner of his mouth down his deathly pale cheek.

Saul whispers in my ear, "Good news is that they think you must be his brother—and I don't blame them. I've gotta say, it's a bit of a shock to see you next to the guy like this. I always thought you had the soul of an angel, but I never..." He looks at me with a quizzical expression, biting his lower lip. Then he shakes his head and continues. "We can talk about that later. Anyway...the bad news is that they already called an ambulance, so we need to get him mobile before the medics arrive...or anyone else."

I hear the urgency in Saul's voice and pick up on his meaning all too well. Demons are almost certainly coming to see what's going on, and we need to be far from here by the time they show up. But how do you administer first aid to an angel? Are the principles the same as for humans? Does he need some special heavenly medicine?

I lean in, placing my lips close to his ear, and say, "Baruchiel? Can you hear me? It's Tom. Can you open your eyes?"

I honestly wasn't expecting any response; I figured the fall had knocked him unconscious. However, to my surprise, there's a slight hitch in his breath and then his eyes flutter open.

"Tom? Not Thomas?"

"Yes. Well, that's what Saul calls me—Tom—and I guess I've gotten used to it." I answer automatically, too taken aback to acknowledge that it's an odd first question from someone who just had a nasty fall.

Baruchiel manages a faint smile. "Tom. I like it."

He tries to sit up and I slip my arm behind his back to support him. It's difficult with his wing in the way, but I manage to get him seated upright. He flaps his wings, forcing me to shift back, and the crowd oohs and ahhs, impressed by the 'costume', still unaware—for now, anyway—that they're the real deal.

"Um...Baruchiel? Are you all right?"

Baruchiel fixes me with a puzzled expression. Then he looks up at the sky. "Ah yes, I fell." He gives another flap of his wings, garnering more excitement from the crowd. "I am well—the impact merely stunned me. I have never fallen before. It is an odd sensation. Rather unpleasant, actually."

"Look, angel, sorry about the fireball and all, but if you're okay, we really need to get off the street."

Saul has manoeuvred himself to the other side of Baruchiel. I look across at him, but his eyes aren't focused on me. They aren't even focused on Baruchiel; his gaze is flitting back and forth over the crowd. In the next breath, he inhales deeply and straight away tenses. He drops to a crouch and grabs Baruchiel's arm, slinging it over his shoulder.

"We have to go, guys! Now!"

Whatever Saul has sensed, Baruchiel must be able to pick up on it, too, because his eyes widen and he nods, struggling to get to his feet. I leap up and grab his other arm, and between us, Saul and I heave him from the horizontal to the vertical plane.

"Can you fly, angel?" I only just catch Saul's question over the clamour of the crowd and the sound of a fast-approaching siren.

"Yes. Alone. Probably. But definitely not with both of you, not quite yet. I need a minute or two to catch my breath first."

The crowd reluctantly parts, a dozen or more cameras flashing, and we forge a path through the vague gap, heading away from the hotel.

"Yeah, yeah, he'll be fine," Saul responds to a query from a bystander. Then he addresses Baruchiel again. "If you can get out of here, scram while you have the chance. Just mask yourself properly from mortal eyes this time. The last thing we need is a tabloid exposé telling all and sundry where we are."

"I cannot leave now. I was sent here to guard Tom's soul."

Saul laughs, but it's not his usual merry chuckle. This one sounds hollow. "Well, you've done a bang-up job so far. Where were you a few months ago when I was seducing him with a cake fork? Where was heavenly intervention when I handed him that parchment and pen?"

"I was only assigned to him yesterday."

"Yesterday? Ha! If Heaven cares so damn much about him, you should've stepped in a hell of a lot sooner than this. Tom's mine now, my responsibility, and I'll do whatever it takes to keep him safe. I'll fry a hundred angels if I have to—you included, if you get in my way."

Things are becoming heated, so I try to interrupt. "Saul, where are we going?"

My question remains unanswered. Saul and Baruchiel are too caught up in their semi-argument, and neither acknowledges me with so much as a glance, let alone a response. Baruchiel's wing is digging into my shoulder blade, but I continue to support him as we stumble across the road and into a small square. In front of us, a statue-lined bridge stretches over a wide river. It's either cross the bridge or double back.

The two of them are still arguing over me. I suppose I should be flattered, but at present it's more of an irritation. Besides, I get the impression that—on Saul's part, anyway—it's less about me per se and more about making a point, claiming a stake, marking his territory. Perhaps I should go and get a tattoo while I wait for them to finish having it out. Big, bold lettering across my chest that reads Tom Ives. Property of Saul. Hands off.

Okay, I confess that, on some subliminal level, the idea of belonging to Saul turns me on. I may be huffing and puffing over his current caveman display, but only because I'm stuck supporting a pretty heavy angel, trying to make a getaway without any idea where we're supposed to be going, and it looks as if I'll have to start all over again with my T-shirt collection, since Saul is unlikely to want to return to the hotel after all that's happened.

"Saul, where are we—"

I don't even get to finish voicing my question this time. My sentence is cut off when a hand comes down heavily on my arm, yanking me backward. I totter, and Baruchiel's wing clips the back of my head as I'm pulled away from him. Considering it's made of feathers, it packs quite a punch, and for a few seconds, I'm seeing stars—and not in the good way. The grip on my arm tightens, becoming painful enough that I cry out. I fumble at the fingers digging into my biceps, trying to pry them loose. It's no good; my assailant is not budging an inch. I turn my head to look at my attacker, ready to yell for help. When I see who—what—I'm dealing with, the words die in my throat.

Chapter Twenty-Six

BARUCHIEL

In any other situation, Baruchiel would have found Saul excessively rude. But suffused as he was with that golden glow, Baruchiel had to acknowledge that Saul's words and actions stemmed from his love for Tom, so he chose not to take offence. Tom. Yes, Baruchiel decided that he liked the sound of it. Tom. The shortened name suited the mortal far better than the formal Thomas. But Saul was talking again and Baruchiel tried to pay attention to the words.

Truth be told, the fall had rather knocked the stuffing out of him. It had been unexpected, and his mind was still trying to play catch-up after its brief but dramatic sojourn into the land of unconsciousness. This mission was providing Baruchiel with a number of new sensations and experiences to catalogue and process: a demon in love, falling from the sky, and now unconsciousness. The first was intriguing, the second had been unpleasant and painful—he shuddered to imagine what it must have been like for those of his brothers who'd fallen all the way into Hell—and the third... Well, since he had no memory of the fall, it was hard to describe, but the aftereffects were certainly disorientating.

It felt strange to have other bodies pressed close to his, arms around him, hands holding him up. But it was somehow comforting, too, and that was why he'd not yet let on that he was feeling more himself and could now walk unassisted. Caught up naming and assessing new sensations and trying to focus on his conversation with Saul at the same time, Baruchiel temporarily forgot the threat at their backs: the faint whiff of brimstone that had begun to seep through the air as they made their way down the street.

When Tom jerked away from him and cried out, it took Baruchiel a moment to regain his balance, nearly taking Saul down with him as he wobbled and beat his wings in an effort to stay on his feet.

"Adramelech."

Saul spat out the name as if it left a bad taste in his mouth, and Baruchiel was in no doubt as to Saul's feelings towards the other demon. Whether it was a long-term feud or merely a result of Hell's pursuit of Tom, there was clearly no love lost between the two of them.

"Saul." Adramelech gave a single nod, but Baruchiel noticed the ghost of a smile, quickly repressed.

"One against three and with mortal bystanders present. The odds are not in your favour today." Saul appeared to have overcome any initial horror at the situation. He lowered his gaze to his hands as he brushed off his suit jacket, straightened his shirt collar, and adjusted his cufflinks.

Adramelech pulled Tom in front of him, and Baruchiel instinctively took a step forward. He halted when a knife materialised in Adramelech's free hand.

With a victorious grin, Adramelech angled the blade towards Tom's neck. "Not another move from either of you." He looked over at Saul. "Odds hardly matter in a situation such as this. You know as well as I do, Saul, he'll be dead before you reach me."

Adramelech gloated, Saul glowered back at him, and Baruchiel noticed a crowd was beginning to gather around them once again. Bright lights flashed intermittently from the small boxes the mortals held. He vaguely recognised a few of the faces from the circle that had surrounded him after his fall. None seemed frightened to find an angel and a demon in their midst. He could only assume they thought this to be some form of street entertainment. He didn't want to see any of them hurt in this altercation, but he couldn't concentrate on everything at once, and for now his priority had to be Tom.

Baruchiel raised his voice. "Adramelech, the matter of Thomas Ives's soul has not yet been decided. Heaven will not take kindly to—"

"The heavenly host can learn to mind its own fucking business."

There came a variety of gasps and laughs from the ever-growing crowd, and more lights flashed in Baruchiel's peripheral vision.

"What are you going to do to me?"

Baruchiel glanced at Tom. He had asked the question in a strong, steady voice, but Baruchiel could see that Tom was shaking; he could see the fear in Tom's eyes.

Adramelech kept his gaze fixed on Saul as he answered. "You and I are taking a little trip below, sweet Tom. That's what he calls you, is it not? Sweet Tom." He shifted his grip to run a hand through Tom's hair, and Baruchiel saw Saul tense and curl his own hands into fists. Adramelech smirked at Saul's reaction and continued. "We're all eager to see what magic you possess that can turn a top-notch demon like Saul here into a mere shadow of his former self." He traced the flat of the blade along Tom's cheek. "I must confess, aside from the angelic appearance, I can't see anything to account for it on the outside. We may well need to go deeper to take a look at what lies beneath the surface."

Saul made a move forward, but Adramelech instantly pressed the tip of the blade over Tom's heart.

"Now, now, Saul. I wouldn't be too hasty if I were you. Knives can be dangerous things—you wouldn't want me to slip. Why don't you just accept the truth? It's over, Saul. You lost. And what did you expect? You alone against all the forces of Hell. How could you ever think you would outrun us?" He cocked his head. "Speaking of which, it looks like the others are here with our transportation." He glanced over at Baruchiel. "I'd fly away, pretty angel. Thomas Ives and Saul are coming with us, and I can guarantee that you don't want to join them."

A gust of wind swept in from nowhere. It buffeted Baruchiel's wings and he had to plant his feet firmly to stay upright. The wind rushed by faster and faster until Baruchiel could see it spinning around them, channelling into a funnel at Adramelech's feet.

"You can't open a portal here, not like this!" Saul yelled over the noise of the gale. "There're humans present, Adramelech. It's against every fucking rule in the book!"

"Special dispensation from the boss," Adramelech hollered back. "To apprehend the two of you, I may use any force and any methods necessary."

Some of the mortals were shrieking now as they scrambled and fought their way out of the square. Baruchiel was aware of their cries, but their voices were so muffled by the wind that they sounded distant and otherworldly. A chasm opened in the pavement. Battered by the pressure of the unnatural storm, the stone cracked and parted, sections of it tumbling into the newly created abyss. Then came the scorching heat.

Looking into the ever-widening pit, Baruchiel could see red-orange flames rising higher and higher, surging towards them. When they reached the top of the chasm, the flames stretched out, sizzling tendrils reaching, searching. They flicked against Adramelech's and Tom's feet and then wrapped tightly around their ankles. The noise and heat combined made it impossible for Baruchiel to hear Tom's scream, but he saw his mouth open in a wide O. A second later, Tom and Adramelech disappeared into the earth.

For a moment, Baruchiel was too stunned to react; it was taking all his residual energy to stay on his feet. Then he noticed a fiery vine working its way towards him, and he flapped his wings, putting some distance between his body and the ground. All he could think was, *I have failed*. Adramelech had taken Tom to Hell right before his eyes and he'd not been able to do a thing to stop it. Even if he'd managed to gather his thoughts in time to try something—and he had no idea what he could've done— a single angel was no match for the demonic forces at work here.

A movement to his right caught his eye and Baruchiel refocused. One of the tendrils had wound its way up Saul's leg and was dragging him towards the chasm. Saul wasn't even trying to resist; he was letting it take him.

Baruchiel's resolve strengthened. He'd missed the opportunity to help Tom, but if he stopped them from gaining Saul, perhaps that would buy him time and offer Heaven some kind of leverage—Hell wanted both the mortal *and* the demon, after all.

He flapped his wings hard and swept down. He reached out and caught hold of Saul's shoulder. With such force battering him, it was hard for Baruchiel to maintain his grip, so he relied on grasping a fistful of Saul's clothing and pulling with all his might.

"What are you doing? Are all you angels this insane?"

Baruchiel chose not to answer. He beat his wings in an attempt to rise, and for a moment, he thought it was going to work. They were gaining ground (or rather air) and the fire's hold on Saul slipped lower, the tendril now only clinging as high as his calf. But then a second flaming vine shot up from the pit. It latched onto Saul's other leg, pulling them back towards the hungry flames and that gaping hole. Baruchiel fought and fought, but he simply wasn't strong enough; he couldn't slow their descent.

"Leave me, angel."

"No, if I can save you—"

"Leave me, damn it. I don't want him to be down there alone."

"But I am supposed to safeguard his soul."

"Then find a way. Fly back to Heaven and find some way to get him out."

Baruchiel hesitated. What Saul was saying was true. He could go home and then return to Hell with a new plan, with reinforcements if necessary. But...

"I said leave me, you thick-skulled moron."

There was a flash of light, the scent of burning fibres, and Baruchiel shot upward so fast he was in danger of spiralling out of control for the second time that day. Then, as suddenly as it had come, the wind stopped. When Baruchiel eventually managed to pull to a halt, he found himself holding a scrap of cloth, the edges charred and still smoking. A brief glance below revealed the hole in the ground was now no more than a black drop into nothing. The portal had closed. Saul and Tom were both in Hell.

Chapter Twenty-Seven

SAUL

The blast of fire I sent into my clothing did its job. I'm in mourning for my favourite Armani suit, but it was the only way. That foolish angel was not letting go, and if I hadn't acted as I did, he'd have been dragged down to Hell, too, and then where would we be? I don't know how much clout one soppy, harebrained angel has, but right now Winged Wonder's my only hope. Or, to be more exact, he's Tom's only hope. If the powers that be up in Heaven can get Tom out of this fix, I'll be content, regardless of what happens to me. I already know I'm beyond saving—I have been for centuries.

The fall to Hell via a portal like that is a long one. As to whether it's a pleasant journey, I guess that depends on the individual. Let's just say, if you're the sort of person who'd puke after a mild merry-go-round ride at the local fair, you wouldn't like it. If, on the other hand, you're a thrill junkie, you might find it rather enjoyable, though a tad on the hot side. It's not dissimilar from a feet-first bungee jump—only a trip to Hell is usually a one-way ticket. There's no safety cord to pull you back up afterward.

Despite the enforced nature of this descent, it's not the first time I've travelled by one of these portals and I manage to land semi-elegantly with only a brief drop to one knee to help absorb the impact. Considering the situation, I'm glad to have kept up appearances by neither landing on my arse nor emptying the contents of my stomach. Rising from my crouch, I dust off what's left of my suit—Oh baby, I'm so sorry!—while casting a surreptitious glance around the room.

As expected, I'm not alone. Far from it. Adramelech's nowhere in sight, but he's been kind enough to organise a welcoming committee. And what a committee! *Ten* demons are apparently needed to handle little old *moi*. Once again, I feel a rush of pride to think that I've inspired such a strong display of force. A quick second sweep, under the auspices of removing ash from my hair, tells me that Tom is as conspicuous by his absence as Adramelech. That's a worry. I experience a surge of panic but fight to suppress it, masking my face with a wide grin as I look openly around the room, nodding to each demon in turn.

"Greetings, boys. Long time no see. I don't suppose any of you want to forget this little misunderstanding and come grab a beer with me topside? First round's on me."

"Quiet, traitor!" The high-pitched squeak comes from a rather squat demon seated on a stool in the corner of the room—a clerk of some sort, judging by the clipboard and pen in his hands. By Satan, I never could stand the paper-pushers.

"Traitor?" I ask, when the appellation registers in my still-tumbling brain. "Come now, I wouldn't go so far as—"

"Silence! The prisoner is denied the right to speak, denied the right to legal representation, and denied the right of appeal, in recognition of the seriousness of his crimes against the realm."

Really? I look around the group, waiting for the burst of laughter that must surely be coming, the acknowledgement that this is merely a joke.

But no one is cracking a smile.

"Seems a bit extreme, don't you think?" I clear my throat. "I mean, it was only one insignificant little soul. It's not like I opened the gates of Hell and let them all out."

I must say, I *am* somewhat taken aback. I didn't expect to be welcomed home with open arms and an open tab at the bar. But a charge of high treason? Then again, such an indictment, the most grievous that can be brought against anyone down here, does make things nice and easy for them. The boss clearly wants this over and done with, swept under the carpet, and what better way to do that than with a speedy trial (I use the term 'trial' loosely) and even swifter sentencing? I had anticipated a lengthy jail time and a major demotion for my misdemeanour; however, it looks like I could be facing something *much* worse. Between you and me, this could very well be the last time we speak—in this lifetime, anyway.

Death is something I haven't had to think about for centuries. After I became a demon, I pretty much assumed I'd live forever. It was part of the role's appeal, after all. When the demon who recruited me made his pitch, that little nugget was the ace up his sleeve, the proverbial dangled carrot: come work for Hell and never die. The brightly hued vegetable hung enticingly in front of my mouth, and believe me, I was more than ready to bite.

England in 1261 was no picnic, I can tell you, and my life was no bed of roses. My own fault. I'd whored and drunk my way through my meagre inheritance, and I spent most of my time staring into the bottom of a cup. The demon found me sitting in a darkened corner in the only place in town where they'd still pour me a draught of ale. He could've offered me a simple, run-of-the-mill deal and no doubt I'd have taken it without a moment's hesitation, but he put a different proposal to me. Hell was doing brisk trade back then, you see. Souls were easy to acquire, practically two-a-penny. What they needed was fresh blood for the workforce.

It was an offer that seemed too good to miss. I figured that I was Hell-bound, anyway, so what did it matter if I went there a few years earlier and on my own terms? I didn't even bother reading through the contract before I put quill to parchment. In retrospect, I guess I should've paid more attention to the small print. But what does it matter now? The past is dead and buried; all I care about is the present. And without Tom, I have no wish to go on. My only remaining desire is to save him before they snuff me out for good.

"You know, I'm thinking that—"

"Save your pathetic excuses for the judge!" The clerk lowers his gaze to his clipboard. "The trial will take place tomorrow morning. Guards, take him to his cell. Adramelech said to use the hottest one available. A touch of Hell-Fire will help him reflect on his numerous and weighty sins."

The two burliest—and smelliest, just my luck—demons in the room grab my arms and drag me backward. I dig in my heels and become a dead weight. No way am I letting them force me from here until I've said my piece. I can't rely on the judge tomorrow letting me offer a defence; this may be the only chance I get to make arrangements for Tom's safety, to have my voice heard. And I do think they're going to be interested in what I have to say.

I clear my throat loudly and the sound makes the guards pause long enough for me to call out, "I wish to make a plea bargain."

The clerk is still scribbling away at his paperwork, but he looks up at my statement. "A plea bargain?" He narrows his eyes and purses his lips. "What exactly are you proposing?"

"I will plead guilty to any and every charge you have on that form of yours. I don't care what it says. I don't need to read it first. I'll happily confess to all and sign my name on the dotted line."

There's a collective gasp from the motley crew surrounding me, and the room erupts into a cacophony of competing voices as everyone present tries to offer an opinion. It *is* quite newsworthy, as it happens. To my knowledge, no one facing our courts has ever pleaded guilty of their own free will before—at least not prior to prolonged bouts of torture.

"In exchange for...?" The clerk has to yell to be heard over the noise.

I raise my voice to ensure all hear me. I want as many witnesses to this as possible. "A full and everlasting renouncement of Hell's claim on the soul of Thomas Ives. In writing, with copies lodged both here and in Heaven."

The hush that falls over the room is so pregnant it almost feels louder than the chorus of voices that had come before. I can sense the weight of ten pairs of eyes all turned on me, and as I look around at the faces of those present, I see quite the gamut of emotions. Some are angry, one or two look awed (I flash those individuals a quick wink), and the others appear somewhat incredulous. Both the guards have let go of my arms; one of them is looking at me as if I've gone insane and he's worried it might be catching. And maybe he's right. Maybe I have lost my mind. Demons don't make noble sacrifices. We don't bargain our lives to save others. But then, we don't fall in love, either.

Now, don't get too excited. I'm still not completely convinced that what I feel for Tom is love. It's been so long since I was human that I can't remember what love felt like anymore. I'm assuming I did feel it once—I must've done, I suppose—but my memories of my mortal life are hazy, to say the least. I have nothing against which to compare what I'm feeling now with the abstract concept I have of love. But even if it's not love, it's the closest I'm ever likely to get to it, and that alone has got to be worth fighting for, don't you agree? Hey, and if I'm truly destined for the chop here, I want to go out with a bang, with a good dose of razzle-dazzle that will leave them talking about me for centuries to come. I'd like to think that young demons will hear my story. Cautionary tale or action romance, I don't care which way they skew it, so long as they never forget my name. Let the boss chew on that! He can kill me if he wants, but I'll remain immortal all the same.

"I-I'm not authorised to make such a deal."

The clerk is looking distinctly edgy—he can't even meet my eye—and I wonder if he, too, believes me to be contagious. I almost feel like yelling my love for Tom for all of Hell to hear. But I resist the urge. I don't want to play all my cards in one go. I may need to keep something in reserve for the trial. Instead, I examine my fingernails for a moment and then stare at the clerk until he's forced to meet my gaze.

"The speedy resolution of a high-profile case like this one would look well on a résumé, wouldn't you say? There'd be the possibility of a promotion or, at the very least, a hefty end-of-year bonus." I pause for a second to let him think on that. Then I add, "If you want a trial so fast it will be a bureaucrat's wet dream, I suggest you find me someone with the necessary authority pronto."

With that, I turn on my heel and stride out of the room, heading towards the holding cells, ready to hunker down and await a visit from Adramelech. The two guards eventually come to their senses and hurry to catch up.

Chapter Twenty-Eight

TOM

The drop seems to go on forever. The heat pummels me as the air rushes past. I lose all sense of time as I fall down, down, ever down. My stomach somersaults, my limbs flail, and my heart pounds so hard I fear it will burst through my chest. All I want is for it to stop. I don't care what such a cessation would mean, what I will have to face afterward; I only pray for this nightmare descent to end.

And then it does.

I hit the ground. Hard. My ankle twists painfully, and I crash to the floor, only just managing to extend my arms in time to save me from a broken nose. I yelp as the heat from the rock beneath me burns my palms, and I struggle to sit up, keeping my bare skin away from contact with the ground.

Someone—something—grabs my arm and hauls me to my feet. I stumble before regaining my balance. My ankle sends jolts of pain shooting up my leg when I try to put any weight on it, but I steady myself as best I can and look into the eyes of the monster who brought me here. He's unlike anything I've ever seen before—more animal than man—and the revulsion, coupled with the physical effects of our roller-coaster journey here, causes bile to rise in my throat. I don't want to show weakness by throwing up, so I swallow it back down, but it leaves a bitter, unpleasant taste in my mouth.

"Welcome to Hell, mortal. My name is Adramelech, and I am your case officer."

The creature's eyes flash and I recognise the strange fire behind them. I've seen it once before, in a restaurant, when a handsome man offered me a deal. *Saul.* I cast a frantic look about me, but the hideous demon and I are the only ones present. There's no sign of my love.

"Where's Saul? What have you done with him?"

"Interesting. I would've thought you'd be far more concerned with your own predicament, sweet Tom."

"Don't call me that. You don't get to call me that."

I start to clench my fists but change my mind and force my fingers to relax, keeping my arms firmly at my sides. Getting angry is not going to help me now. Even if I *could* beat this guy in a fight—and I seriously doubt that, seeing as the closest I've ever come to violence in the past was the squashing of a cockroach, over which I'm still a little traumatised—what would I do next? I know I'm in Hell, but I don't know whereabouts, and I don't know what's happened to Saul. I wouldn't have a clue how to get out of this room, let alone find my way home. Even assuming a return to Earth is within the realms of possibility and not wishful thinking.

Adramelech smirks as he watches me work through my inner battle, but then his expression clouds into a glower and there's a harsh edge to his words when he speaks again. "You're in our domain now, boy, and I can call you whatever I wish." He steps closer and it takes all my willpower not to shrink back. "Not only that, I can *do* anything to you I wish, and no one would blink an eye. A spell cloaks this room in silence, but if I were to strip that away, you'd hear the cries of your fellow men—all the other fools like you who made deals with the devil and are now paying the price for their avarice, their lust. The rules are clear and inviolable. You signed the contract of your own free will and now your soul is ours."

"You're right. I did sign freely and I don't dispute your claim, but..." At my words, Adramelech raises his eyebrow. The motion is accompanied by a rustle of tattered, dirt-encrusted feathers, and I momentarily lose my train of thought as I stare at them.

"But what? Are you going to try to bargain for your life, for your soul, sweet Tom?" He emphasises the term of endearment and I grit my teeth. On *his* lips the pet name sounds vile, polluted. Desecrated.

"No, I want to bargain for Saul." The look of surprise on Adramelech's face appears to be genuine. "Where is he? What will happen to him?"

Adramelech recovers his composure and offers a smile—one for which I do not much care. "Saul stands accused of high treason. He's being escorted to a cell as we speak and will face trial in the morning."

"And the likely sentence?" Even as I ask the question, my heart sinks and my stomach knots.

Adramelech laughs. "Come now, surely you're not *that* naïve? In your world, what's the usual punishment for such a heinous crime?"

"Lifelong imprisonment?" I offer this more in hope than in any belief it's the correct answer.

"Try again."

"Not death?"

He gives a single nod and widens his grin.

"But I thought...that is, I got the impression that demons are immortal."

Actually, it's not something Saul and I have ever discussed. I'd like to say it was because we were on the run and didn't have time for such debates, but that would only be half the truth. I think, when it came down to it, neither of us wanted to dwell on how impossible our relationship really was…is…was. Being on the run was what made 'us' possible, because all the while we were concentrating on that, we could ignore the fact that our lives were incompatible. Suppose Hell had turned a blind eye and let us get away with breaking the contract—we would then have had to address the issue that he and I have very different life expectancies, that he will stay young, handsome and perfect forever, whereas I will wither and die.

"In essence, you're right. No mortal can kill us, no matter what method they try. And, by Hell, we had fun watching them attempt it again and again in Russia a few years back. About a century ago, a group of humans set their sights on one of my colleagues, who happened to be masquerading as a spiritual leader at the time. They used all manner of diverse and often highly imaginative methods to rid themselves of him. It did no good, of course, and they became more and more terrified with each failed attempt. Ah, those were the days…" Adramelech stares at a spot on the wall over my shoulder, no doubt reviewing some old memory, but a moment later, he resumes as if he'd never trailed off. "However, Hell creates demons—it's a process we all go through when we're recruited—and what can be done can be undone. Once Saul is mortal again, it will be the easiest thing in the world to take his life. So simple, as it happens, that I'm sure many of my brethren will find it anticlimactic."

I close my eyes. I don't care if that makes me look weak. I couldn't give a fig what this demon thinks of me. Saul's death is on me. *I'm* the reason he broke the contract. I know he believes he's to blame for seducing me into signing in the first place, but I lured him every bit as much as he lured me. Not knowingly, not with any kind of malicious intent, but I led him to abandon his work and turn his back on his old life all the same. *I* made him a traitor.

I gulp down the saliva that's gathered at the back of my throat and open my eyes. Adramelech is watching me closely, another smirk twisting his lips into a cruel half smile. I lift my chin and meet his gaze, squaring my shoulders.

"What will it take to commute Saul's sentence?"

"Nothing *you* have the power to provide, little human. The boss is determined on this one, and so am I. Saul has made Hell look foolish, lowered our image in the eyes of Heaven and Earth alike, and that cannot be allowed to go unpunished, lest others get it into their heads that they, too, can flout the rules without consequence. Order would descend into chaos and then where would we be?" He shakes his head. "You have nothing to offer me, Thomas Ives. Unlike gullible Saul, I'm not interested in your body"—inwardly, I breathe a sigh of relief to know anything of that nature is off the cards. I'll do whatever it takes to save Saul, but even so, the mere thought of it...with him... I can't repress a shudder—"and you can hardly hand yourself over in exchange for his freedom when you're already caught."

"What about another deal? You get my soul right now, no waiting."

Adramelech laughs even louder than before. The sound echoes around the cavernous chamber, and despite the gravity of the situation, I can't help but think it impressive that so many movies got it right: apparently villains *do* laugh in that deep, throaty way, the sound all but overwhelming the room.

"This is why I suggested you should consider your own situation when we first arrived. You've been so busy worrying about your precious Saul that you've failed to ask the most pertinent question: What's going to happen to *me* now? Well, I'm sorry to say, sweet Tom, that the breaking of a contract is a serious matter indeed—as serious to you as a count of high treason is to Saul. Any deal you made with Saul is null and void. Your life is ours now, and we intend to take it, and with it your soul. Tomorrow you'll appear at Saul's trial. After that, you will be executed and your soul will be given over to Hell's finest. I can assure you that they will rip screams from you far louder and more heartfelt than any Saul brought forth when he shared your bed."

Adramelech strides across the room. He waves his hand at the wall and the rock melts away in a shimmer of red light. Then he turns back to face me.

"I would get some rest, if I were you, while you have this final chance to experience peaceful slumber. Oh, and one other thing." He drags out the moment. "Whatever Saul professed to feel for you, it was all a sham. Demons can't love; it's impossible. It was sex for him, nothing more. The fact that he stayed with you so long says something for your prowess between the sheets, though, and I'll pass that information to my colleagues when they take charge of your soul. I'm sure they'll be able to draw some inspiration from it. Now, enjoy your night, *sweet Tom*." With that, he disappears through the opening, and once the red light fades, the wall is back in place.

Adramelech's lying. Of course he's lying. Demons lie. But Saul's a demon. Does that mean Saul would lie to me? No, why would he? He's never told me that he loves me, anyway, so he can't have been lying about it. Unless that in itself answers the question. Did he never say the words because he doesn't love me, *can't* love me? That would make sense. And yet, why risk everything to run away with me the way he did? If all he cared about was sex, he could have let the contract stand. I was already offering him a new deal that would have ensured him plenty of nights in my bed without having to break a single rule. No, Adramelech's taunting me, playing with me. Saul cares for me; I have to believe that. I *want* to believe that. God, do I want to believe it.

My ankle is throbbing, so I sink to the floor and pull my legs in, hugging them tight against my chest, resting my chin upon my knees. Whether or not this is the last night of my life, I know I won't sleep a wink. Tomorrow is the trial. There's still a chance Saul will be acquitted, that his life will be spared. Even as I think it, I know it's a pipe dream. Adramelech made it pretty clear that this trial is merely for show; the verdict and sentence have already been decided. Saul is condemned no matter what manner of defence he tries to mount.

That thought makes my eyes sting, but I blink away the threatening tears, knowing that if I allow them to start flowing, they will never stop. There's only one way I'm going to make it through this night without driving myself mad with worry and sorrow. I close my eyes and try to forget where I am, what's in store. I turn instead to the past and lose myself in happy memories of the last few months. Just me and Saul. Together. As we were meant to be.

Chapter Twenty-Nine

BARUCHIEL

Baruchiel had not wasted a moment. As soon as it was clear the portal had gone and was not coming back, he had spread his tired, aching wings once more and taken to the skies, heading up and up until layers of thick, grey-white cloud shielded him from mortal view. Despite how many years he'd been away from the earthly realm, it hadn't taken him long to find the once-familiar path that would guide him back to Heaven. And now here he was...waiting.

He worried at his left thumbnail as he continued to stare at the closed gate that shimmered on the other side of the cloud on which he was seated. The angel standing guard outside the entranceway looked straight ahead, but Baruchiel had not failed to notice the occasional glances his brother threw his way. Baruchiel was unsure if it was the nature of the urgent message he'd sent that had caused the fellow such consternation or whether it was the fact that Baruchiel had spent the last half hour biting every one of his nails down to the quick. Strange, mortal-like habits such as nail biting were not something in which angels usually indulged—he had never once done it before today—but the wait was driving him to distraction, and it was the only way he'd been able to steady himself.

What is taking so long? Surely the archangels have made a decision by now. Baruchiel could feel the weight of every passing second bearing down upon him, ominous and heavy. How long had Tom and Saul been trapped down there? What was happening to them? By the time he reached them, would it already be too late? These questions whirled around and around in his mind until he wanted to scream. Had he been alone, he probably would have done so. But the presence of his brother held him in check. The other angel already regarded his behaviour as strange; the last thing Baruchiel needed was to reinforce that belief. He didn't want to be pulled from this mission. Not now.

There was a gentle tinkling of bells, followed by a trumpet fanfare, and the gate slowly swung open. Baruchiel hurried forward, dropped to his knee, and bowed his head as the archangel Gabriel emerged.

"Baruchiel, is it not?"

Baruchiel looked up and nodded.

"I apologise for keeping you waiting, Brother, but this situation is a complex one and no mistake. It has taken us time to discuss the options and consider what may be done."

"And have you now reached a decision?" Baruchiel held his breath and fought against the urge to fidget, determined not to show any un-angelic qualities in front of his superior.

Gabriel nodded. "Heaven's lawmakers have confirmed that, since one of their own broke the contract, the demons no longer have a claim on Thomas Ives's soul and they, therefore, had no right to drag him down to Hell. He belongs to us once again and you may enforce this, knowing that you have the full might of Heaven behind you. Go back to Hell, good Baruchiel, and make this right." He held out a scroll. "The paperwork is all in order, so Lucifer can make no quarrel as to its authenticity. Hand them this and then return Thomas Ives to Earth."

"And Saul? What of Saul?"

"Saul?" Gabriel's brow furrowed. "Oh, you mean the demon." He paused. "We did discuss his case, but I am afraid his legal situation is also clear. Saul is a demon and belongs to Hell. As such, Heaven cannot interfere on his behalf. You must leave him to his fate."

"But he loves Tom, and Tom loves him."

"That is not possible."

"Gabriel, I swear it is true. I have seen the heaven-bright glow of their love with my own eyes." Gabriel's frown deepened; Baruchiel pressed on. "Is that not the reason Heaven was so keen to save Tom?"

"No." Gabriel cast a look at the angel by the gate and then inched closer to Baruchiel, lowering his voice. "Thomas Ives is...family."

Baruchiel followed Gabriel's lead and kept his voice to a whisper. "But Heaven would not usually interfere for a half-breed."

"His parentage is...loftier than usual for a nephilim. That is all I can say." He finished with a pointed look and a slight jerk of his head in the direction of the gate.

Ah, now it was clear. It would seem that one of the archangels had suffered a momentary lapse of chastity when last down amongst the mortals. No wonder Heaven was so keen to keep Thomas Ives out of Hell. If the demons discovered his parentage, they'd have a field day. Why, the propaganda value alone...!

Baruchiel nodded his understanding and Gabriel turned to go.

Without thinking, Baruchiel grabbed Gabriel's sleeve. "But Saul?"

"I am sorry, Brother, but we cannot interfere in demon justice. To do so could prompt all-out violence between our two realms, the likes of which we have not seen in over a thousand years. That is too great a price to pay for a single life, especially when the life in question is that of a soul-scamming, unrepentant demon." He shook his head. "But you must hurry back to Hell now, Baruchiel. Go and reclaim Thomas Ives while there is still time."

Baruchiel's throat felt tight and he did not trust himself to speak, so he simply nodded his acquiescence and bowed as Gabriel walked back towards the gate. He was already at the edge of the cloud, spreading his wings to fly, when Gabriel called out to him.

"I am Heaven's messenger, Baruchiel, and that function I *can* perform on behalf of your demon. I make no promises, but I will relay the information you have provided to the others and will see what they have to say on the matter." He paused. "Just make certain that Thomas Ives remains your priority. Ensure his safety before any other considerations."

With that, Gabriel slipped back through the doorway, and the shining golden gate eased shut behind him, leaving Baruchiel alone with the guard, who was sporting a practiced, blank expression as he stared resolutely ahead. Baruchiel didn't envy the angel his job one bit. How dull it must be to stand there all day opening and closing a gate, barely acknowledged except as a pair of ears constituting a potential security threat. Offering the guard a friendly smile—which wasn't returned—Baruchiel leapt off the cloud.

The scroll tucked into his robes filled Baruchiel with joy. Thomas Ives would soon be free of Hell's clutches, and Baruchiel would see him safely back home, having successfully fulfilled his mission. A decisive victory here could well see him sent on future assignments. Being out and about in the realms again these past couple of days had reminded him how much he missed his old work, and he longed to continue it, regardless of the ravages to his outfit and his recent collision with the ground. His thoughts strayed and he wondered briefly which of the archangels had been the one to succumb to the charms of Tom's mother. But that hardly mattered. Whoever it was, the secret needed to be kept, the unfortunate lapse forever hidden from prying eyes.

Baruchiel knew he should be content with this outcome, which met all the requirements of his initial instructions, but thoughts of Saul marred his happiness. Yes, Saul was a demon and, yes, he had seduced Tom and countless others into signing away their souls. Yet, he was unique—a demon in love. Not to mention the fact that Tom would take his loss very badly indeed. And wasn't Baruchiel's mission to protect Tom's soul from harm? Did that not include warding against heartbreak and despair? *If it were up to me, I would save the demon. I would find a way.* But it wasn't up to him. The archangels had spoken and Baruchiel had no choice but to obey, whether he liked it or not.

When Baruchiel reached the mortal realm, he continued into the depths of the earth. It was not long before he stood again in front of Hell's gates. The same demon gatekeeper as before answered his knock, greeting him with a sneer and a dollop of spittle that landed close to his feet.

Undeterred by the disrespectful welcome, Baruchiel stepped forward and opened the scroll for the demon to see. "I am here on behalf of Heaven, as you see." He rolled up the scroll and placed it back within his robes.

"Adramelech's busy with the trial." The demon spat again and bared his teeth. "Come back tomorrow, pretty boy."

A trial! What if I have come too late? Fighting to keep his expression neutral, Baruchiel knocked the surprised demon aside and forced his way into the realm of the damned. When the gate closed behind him, Baruchiel turned to the demon and let his full power blaze behind his eyes.

"I do not care what he is doing. I demand to see Adramelech right this minute. Refuse my request again and you will have more than one angel to contend with this day. Unless you wish to unleash war on us all, I suggest you take me to this trial."

Chapter Thirty

SAUL

I lounge in the dock and survey the gathering—it's quite a crowd! I overheard one of the guards say that they'd had to raffle tickets because half of Hell had been intent on attending the 'trial of the century'. Good to know I'm at least as popular as Charles Guiteau! Although, unlike Charlie-boy, I have no illusions that I'll be heading up to Heaven at the end of this. Oh, and in case you're interested, yes, Charlie did come down here to us. He got a reprieve after a year though. We tired of his constant jabbering, so we decided to let the angels deal with him instead. He's their problem now, thank the Devil.

Anyhow... I assume from the cameras set up around the room that proceedings will be broadcast to those unlucky in the ticket allocation. Hell, if I'd known I'd be on display to so many, I'd have requested a fresh, unsinged suit. Then again, my handsomely ragged appearance does rather add to the drama, I suppose. What do you think? Could I be cast as the freedom fighter? The antihero? Not if Adramelech has his way, I'm sure. However, public opinion and official opinion are sometimes two very different things. To the populace, I may well become Hell's answer to Che Guevara.

The door at the back melts open and in strolls Adramelech. He's looking very dapper, I must say; the guy even washed his feathers for the occasion. No doubt the boss will be watching the feed and Adramelech wants to make a good impression. Perhaps he hopes a strong performance here will bump him back up the ranks. Well, bully for him. At his arrival, everyone stands, but I make no attempt to straighten. I just throw him a mock salute that elicits a scowl. No need to be concerned that I'm jeopardizing my trial—it's all part of the act. Adramelech and I came to terms last night. We struck a gentlemen's agreement and all this is nothing more than a show to keep up appearances.

"Please be seated." Adramelech exudes authority today. He barely waits for a hush to descend before continuing. "We are here to try the defendant, Saul, who stands accused of high treason." An excited murmur from the crowd—oh, they are loving the drama! "Saul, I put it to you that you did knowingly destroy a legally binding contract in an attempt to deny Hell its rightful claim on the soul of one Thomas Ives. And, further, that you did collude with said Thomas Ives to flee from just punishment for this crime. How do you plead?"

Collude? The word troubles me. It marks Tom as an accomplice, and that's not what I agreed to last night. But maybe I'm being paranoid. It could well be that Adramelech merely got caught up in the moment and was trying to make his speech sound as fancy as possible for the cameras. Besides, I don't have many options right now. I'll have to go along with it.

"Guilty as charged."

The hubbub in the room is so thrilling a smile creeps onto my lips. I see a camera lens pointed towards me and I widen my grin, giving the viewers a flash of my pearly whites. Regardless of how this trial ends, I can at least bow out knowing that I've given my fellow demons one damn fine performance. Denizens of Hell, I am ready for my close-up.

Adramelech pounds his gavel against the desk with such force that I hear the wood splinter, the sound obvious even over all the noise in the room. I know you'd think wood would be a bad idea in a fiery realm like ours, but what can I say? Wood is aesthetically pleasing. And as I've told you before, we demons do love our luxuries. It dries out pretty badly down here, though, so we're constantly nabbing new items during our trips topside. But I digress...

The forceful gavelling did its job and a semblance of order has returned to the chamber. The anticipation in the air is palpable. I can almost taste it on the tip of my tongue. And I can certainly feel it brush over my skin, making the hairs at the back of my neck jump to attention.

"The defendant admits his guilt and sentence will be passed shortly. First, bring out the second prisoner."

Something is wrong. Something is very, very wrong. This is not what I was promised last night. Adramelech assured me that Tom would be kept out of it, that he'd have already returned topside by the time this trial commenced. His freedom for my compliance. That was the deal I proposed, and Adramelech agreed to it. He shook my hand. We made a pact.

My worst fears are realised when the doorway opens and someone shoves Tom through. From the reaction of several of the older members of the crowd, I'm guessing a few of them have seen an angel before. They've noted Tom's appearance and they've already formed certain conclusions. Mere seconds after his arrival, I hear the word 'angel' whispered somewhere behind me, and the spectators' excitement ratchets up another notch.

Tom stumbles forward. He's leaning heavily to one side, keeping his weight off his left foot, and my gaze drops to his swollen ankle. He's injured. Rage bubbles in the pit of my stomach, sweeping aside fear and worry. How dare they touch him, hurt him! He looks up and catches my eye, and I don't like what I read in his expression. He's resigned, defeated. Clearly he's been told something I haven't—and whatever it was, it wasn't good.

I swing around to face Adramelech. The vicious smile on his face confirms what I suspected the moment he called Tom in here: I've been played. That bastard has no intention of honouring our deal. He never did. I don't know why I'm surprised—demons are not known for their honesty and fair play—but I'd hoped...

What else could I have done? The deal I thought I'd made with this fiend was my only chance to save Tom, so I took it and convinced myself it would all work out, because *not* having that belief would have driven me to madness.

Adramelech turns from me, looking excessively pleased with himself, and transfers his attention to Tom. "Thomas Ives. You stand here accused of several serious crimes."

He peers down at his paperwork as if he needs to check the items before listing them. He drags the moment out, overacting like hell, shaking his head as if he cannot believe what he's reading, cannot conceive of the horrendous crimes that have been committed. It makes me want to storm over there and punch his lights out. The crowd, on the other hand, is lapping it up. Finally, he looks up, gazing first at me and then turning to Tom as he reads the charges. His words reverberate around the chamber.

"The charges are as follows: breach of contract, resisting arrest, and"—he pauses to cast another gleeful glance my way—"subversion of a demon."

What? Whoever heard of such a fucking ridiculous charge?

There are oohs and ahhs from the audience, who, it seems, cannot believe their luck to be present for such an historical event. Well, screw them. Screw them all. This isn't right. It's not just. Yeah, yeah, I know it sounds odd for a demon to care about justice, but this isn't work, it's personal...and both Tom and I have been royally fucked over.

"In light of these heinous acts, the accused's life and soul are forfeit. He is hereby condemned to death and we will carry out the sentence immediately." Adramelech gestures to one of the guards. "Call forth the executioner."

No, no, no, no, no. This isn't happening. This can't be happening. Tom's going to die, right here, right now, before my very eyes. I can't watch that. I can't. Let them burn me, torture me, kill me; I'll take everything they can throw at me. But I can't stand here, impotent, unable to save him, forced to watch as the light leaves his eyes and his lifeless body crumples.

I *won't* watch it. I have to stop them. I have to save him.

I surge out of the dock towards Adramelech, my hands already clenched into fists, fire heating my palms. I barely make it halfway across the floor before one of the guards tackles me to the ground. Another jumps on me and then a third, and I don't have the strength to shake them off. They drag me up, pulling me back to the dock. The crowd has erupted and I have to yell at the top of my voice to be heard over the ruckus.

"Adramelech! You double-crossing bastard. You promised me. We had a deal. We shook hands on it. We had a deal, dammit!"

Adramelech descends from his bench. The guards hold me in place as he leans in to whisper in my ear.

"Oh Saul, I'm merely following the precedent you set. If *you* can break deals whenever the mood takes you, so can I. For too long I've stood by, watching you garner the boss's favour while I, who had served him faithfully for so many years, found myself relegated to demeaning paperwork, shut away in a dark room, all my great deeds of the past forgotten. Presiding over your fall from grace brings me more delight than you could ever comprehend, and the crowning moment will be the look on your face when I snuff out your sweet Tom's life and hand over his soul to the corrections team."

There's a hum of anticipation from the crowd and I look up to see the executioner standing in the doorway. I struggle against the guards, but their grip on me is unyielding. There's nothing I can do but watch through—I willingly confess—fast-moistening eyes as the demon advances towards Tom.

Chapter Thirty-One

TOM

How many hours I've been here now, I couldn't say. This room is cut off from everything, offering no way to mark the time. My ankle still throbs. It's puffy and I've had to remove my trainers to accommodate the swelling. Only my socks remain to guard my skin against the heat coming from the rock beneath me, and I raise each foot for a few seconds every now and again to relieve the worst of the burn and to stop the cotton from sizzling away.

I suppose I'm resigned. That's probably the best word for it. I don't *want* to die, but I can see no way out of this mess, for either Saul or myself, so I'm doing my best not to dwell on what might have been. Signing that contract was my choice. Allowing Saul to destroy it and going on the run with him—also my decision. I don't hold a grudge. Not even against that creepy feathered guy. If I have one regret, it's that Saul and I couldn't hold out a little longer. It would have been wonderful if we could have had a handful of additional weeks together, even a single day, an hour, before...

Since meeting Saul, my life has taken on something of a fantasy tinge. A few times in the early days of our flight, I wondered if I were dreaming all this. Perhaps I'd been hit by a bus and was lying in hospital in a coma, inventing myself a comic-book existence as my mind struggled to reconnect with my body. Is Saul merely a figment of my imagination? Because surely he's too perfect to be real. Surely I couldn't have been *that* lucky?

In my old life, I was a no-one, invisible to all but a handful of my work colleagues, dealing with the double whammy of being an all-out nerd and gay to boot. Then along came Saul. And he saw me, really saw me. When he looks at me, I feel like I'm a part of something, complete. His expression is always one of wonder, adoration, and desire. How could that be possible? How could that be anything but a fantasy produced by a desperate mind?

And yet, if my coma theory were true, this would be the moment when the hero sweeps in. Someone would have appeared by now and whisked us away to safety. Since that hasn't happened, I can only assume that, as crazy as all this seems, it's one hundred percent real. And soon Saul and I will be one hundred percent dead.

A scraping noise startles me out of my reverie and I look up to see the doorway melting in a crimson haze. The demon—I assume he's another demon—who beckons me looks human, unlike the last one. He's a burly fellow, real boxer material, and I decide against attempting anything rash. I struggle to my feet, stretching my tired, cramped muscles, and hobble after him down a long, dark corridor. If they were going for 'ominous deathtrap' when they constructed this hallway, they nailed it.

When the demon reaches another doorway, he opens it with a wave of his hand and pushes me through. Caught off guard by my violent ingress, I stumble, and it takes me a moment to get my bearings. The room is packed and there's a definite buzz in the air. I feel eyes on me and look around. Then I see Saul. He looks stricken, and in that moment, I want nothing so much as to run to him and throw myself into his arms. But I hold back, certain these demons won't permit me to make it that far unimpeded, not wanting to make things any worse than they already are.

"Thomas Ives. You stand here accused of several serious crimes."

The words wash over me. I'm aware of them, I hear them, but I'm not really taking them in. All the strength I can summon I dedicate to looking at Saul, drinking him in for what will more than likely be the last time. I want to remember him perfectly after I die. Whatever they do to my soul, I want to be able to cling to the memory of him. Because it was worth it. God, was it worth it.

When Adramelech reads the charges, Saul's reaction is instantaneous. I don't know what deal he thinks he made, but clearly it's been broken. From the violence of his reaction, I can only assume it had something to do with *my* fate. Did he try to save me? One look at him, at the wild terror in his eyes, tells me this was indeed the case and the thought brings me some comfort. It doesn't matter that he failed. The fact that he tried proves, once and for all, that Adramelech was wrong: Saul *does* love me. I smile at him, wanting to reassure him that it's okay, that I don't blame him. But he's not looking at me anymore.

I follow the line of his gaze and see the executioner in the doorway. For a second my courage fails and all I can think is that I don't want to die. I can feel the sudden hike of my pulse in the hammering of my heart, the rushing of blood in my ears, and I'm ready to either sink to the floor in a quivering heap or make a run for it; I'm not sure which. Summoning an extreme burst of willpower, I push both impulses aside and hold my ground, determined to stay strong for Saul, if not for myself. He'll doubtless blame himself for my death as it is; I don't want to make it any worse for him.

I lift my chin and take a resolute step forward. I wonder if I'm supposed to kneel or bow my head, but no one has issued any such instruction, so I remain upright, shoulders back and chest open. The executioner—who is dressed in long black robes, no less—raises a gleaming scythe. He looks every bit the Grim Reaper of myth, and I wonder if that's intentional or whether it's a coincidence. The hum of the crowd drops to a steady murmur of anticipation, the executioner prepares to swing the blade, I close my eyes, and then...

"Stop! Thomas Ives belongs to Heaven."

I recognise the voice at once and twist to peer towards the back of the hall.

Baruchiel stands in the open doorway, brandishing a scroll. Someone in the audience claps and cheers at his arrival, but I'm uncertain if this bystander is pleased at the turn of events, happy to see me saved from the blade, or simply eager for an escalation and prolongation of the drama.

"You! What are you doing here?" Adramelech marches towards Baruchiel, looking far from content with this development.

"Adramelech, I have here paperwork from Heaven which proves, beyond a shadow of a doubt, that Thomas Ives's soul belongs to us." Baruchiel holds out a rolled parchment and Adramelech snatches it from his hand. "Surrender Tom to me at once. If you refuse, the full might of Heaven will be on your doorstep before you can blink."

Adramelech peruses the paperwork and his brow furrows into a mild frown that fast develops into a full-on scowl. He looks across at me. Then he turns back to Baruchiel.

"The paperwork is in order, angel. Take him and get out of here. Just don't let me see your face around here ever again."

Baruchiel beckons to me and holds out his hand, but I stand immobile, not quite believing what just happened. Had Baruchiel not arrived when he did, had he entered a few seconds later, that vicious-looking blade would've passed through my neck. Talk about a *deus ex machina*! I was about to die and now...I'm not. I'm alive. I'm alive, and I'm being set free. Relief floods through me and my heart leaps. It's over. We're saved.

I step forward and take Baruchiel's hand. He smiles down at me, but there's something hesitant in his expression, something guarded. When the truth sinks in, all my joy at deliverance vanishes. Baruchiel only said *my* name when he entered the room; he didn't mention Saul. This reprieve is not for both of us. Baruchiel is only here to rescue me.

I turn to look at my love. Saul's still in the dock, still restrained. He offers me a smile tinged with sadness and a nod that I take to mean that he wants me to go, to leave him. But I can't. He tried to save me. How can I not return the favour? How can I walk out of here knowing I'm leaving him to die?

"What about Saul?" I ask the room at large.

The chamber is so quiet you probably *could* hear a pin drop. It feels like no one's breathing. Everyone's waiting to see how this will play out. And none more so than I.

"The paperwork said nothing of Saul," Adramelech screeches. "Take the mortal if you must, but Saul is ours to punish."

Baruchiel looks down at me, regret clearly written on his face. "I am sorry, Tom, but Heaven has no sway over demon justice. There is nothing we can do to help him."

"Go, sweet Tom. Get out of here," Saul says before I can raise an objection. "Go live your life and forget about me. Just promise me you'll never make another deal. Promise me that, Tom, and I'll be able to face the end happily enough, knowing you're safe, knowing that no demon will ever get his claws into you again."

"I won't leave you to die alone, Saul." I can feel tears brewing behind my eyes, and I try to hold them back. "I'll stay until the end."

"Enough of this sentimental nonsense." Adramelech snarls and Baruchiel tightens his grip on my hand. "Stay for the show by all means, but I want both of you gone the second his lifeless body hits the ground."

I open my mouth to speak, but this time it's Baruchiel who beats me to it.

"We will comply."

Adramelech offers a grimace. Then he turns back to address the rest of the room. "This court acknowledges the defendant's guilty plea and his sentence will now be proclaimed." He looks at Saul. "The penalty for your crimes is death. Your powers will be stripped from you and your residual mortal life will be terminated, after which your immortal soul will remain in Hell for all eternity, to suffer whatever torments we see fit to inflict. Bring out the mage!"

A robed figure enters the room and moves to stand in front of Saul. The three demons still hold him in place, but I notice they edge back as far as they can without letting go of him. Whatever this guy is about to do to Saul, it's bad enough to worry these three hellish creatures, and that thought makes me bite down on my tongue hard enough that I taste blood.

Saul, I love you.

I want to call it out, to let him hear me say it one last time, but my voice doesn't seem to want to obey me. My parched throat is so tight I can scarcely breathe, let alone speak.

In the next heartbeat, the robed demon begins to chant.

Chapter Thirty-Two

BARUCHIEL

The dark power in the room grew stronger as the figure chanted. Baruchiel could feel it in the air around him: a heavy, malevolent presence that set the feathers in his wings aflutter. He wanted nothing more than to drag Tom from that cursed place and get them both back above ground. But Tom needed this final moment with his lover, and Baruchiel believed he owed him that much, since he'd failed to find a way to save Saul from his awful fate.

The chanting was louder now, but it didn't drown out the cry that erupted from Saul's lips. He sank to his knees, and those holding him released their grip and scurried back. Everyone in the room stared at Saul as he scrunched his eyes shut and twisted his head from side to side. Some watched with glee, but a few looked decidedly uneasy, a gleam of terror evident in their eyes.

Saul screamed again, and Tom's grip on Baruchiel's hand became painfully tight. Not that Baruchiel planned to say anything or extract himself. All the while Tom was holding on to him, he wasn't dashing forward, trying to get to Saul. Paperwork or no paperwork, should Tom get it into his head to interfere in Saul's sentence, Baruchiel wasn't certain he'd be able to get him out of there alive.

The robed figure ended his chant with a flourish of his hands, and this time it was not a cry that he dragged from Saul's throat. An invisible force flung Saul backward and pinned him in place. His arms spread wide, every muscle tensed, fists clenched; his eyes stared, their gaze frantic; and his lips parted in a silent scream.

Baruchiel had never seen anything like it before, but he could sense what was happening. The spark within Saul, the essence that made him a demon, was being ripped away. The mage's spell was forcing through bones and muscles and veins the black magic that had permeated his every cell, drawing the strands together, winding them into a tight ball, channelling the power out of him. Baruchiel could see the flaming red-black sphere hovering within Saul's chest, pushing towards his throat. A few lingering, painful seconds passed, and then...

Fire burst forth from Saul's mouth and eyes, huge spurts of flame that leapt skyward with a crackle and a hiss. Dark power resided in that fire, burning away every drop of black magic until nothing was left. In the next breath, the flames vanished and Saul slumped, crashing to the floor.

There was a flash of movement to the left and Baruchiel saw the executioner take a step towards the fallen ex-demon, raising his blade.

"Saul! No!"

Tom broke free before Baruchiel realised what was happening, but he flapped his wings for momentum and managed to grab Tom's arm before he could break through the crowd to reach his lover.

"Let go of me, Baruchiel. Saul needs me. I can't just—"

"Tom. Stop." Saul's voice was weak and rasping, but it was loud enough to capture Tom's attention and make him break off.

"But, Saul..."

"Let it be, Tom. I've lived long enough, and I've done enough damage to warrant a hundred deaths and centuries of torment."

Baruchiel felt a tear form in the corner of his eye. The unexpected bead of moisture ran down his cheek and splashed onto his spotless white robes. If only Heaven could have found a way to save Saul too. It seemed so unfair.

"Enough! Executioner, do your job." Adramelech waved his hand at the scythe-wielding demon and then sneered at Saul. "Any final words from the condemned? If so, I suggest you make them quick."

"I love him."

Adramelech's sneer morphed into a frown. "What did you say?"

Saul forced himself up off the floor, steadying himself on his knees. "I said that I love him." He turned to Tom. "I love you, Tom, sweet boy. Forgive me, please, and then forget me. I am truly, truly sorry. For everything."

The executioner swung the scythe.

But it never struck its mark.

Suddenly, a brilliant white light drenched the room. It was so pure and so bright that even Baruchiel had to shield his eyes against its glow. When it finally cleared, a new figure stood centre stage, reviewing the scene, his mouth set in a thin line and a gleaming silver sword held by his side, its tip pointing towards his sandal-clad feet.

Baruchiel rubbed his eyes, unsure if what he was seeing was real or if the dramatic events of recent days had finally taken their toll on his sanity. "Michael?"

"Ah, Baruchiel, you *are* here. That is good. Gabriel told me I would find you in this stinking, godforsaken place." He paused to sniff, screwing up his face in distaste.

"However, I worried that you would already be gone by the time I arrived. I have come to tell you that we have given careful consideration to your request on behalf of the demon, Saul, and—"

"No, no, no, no, no!" Adramelech stormed across the room, waving his arms. "You have no business here, angel. We had no choice but to relinquish Thomas Ives, in light of the argument you presented, but that's as far as it goes. Take him." He pointed a bony finger at Baruchiel. "Take the boy, and get out of here. You have no jurisdiction over Hell's justice system and no claim on Saul. He's one of us."

Michael looked down his nose at Adramelech and the gesture gave Baruchiel a good deal of satisfaction. Probably more than was suitable for a forgiving and compassionate angel, but he'd analyze that later.

Lowering his gaze, Michael examined his sword, twisting the blade back and forth in his hand. "A few moments ago, what you say was true. But things have changed. Saul is no longer a demon—you made him mortal again. That was your first mistake. You then committed a second grievous error of judgment when you invited him to speak."

Michael turned his gaze to Saul, an amused half smile lighting his face. "I must say, it is a first for us to come across a demon capable of love, but my brother here was right in his assessment. The truth of it is clear for all angel-kind to see. In the last moments of your life, you had no thought for yourself, only for Thomas Ives. You have asked for forgiveness, Saul, and Heaven is both willing and able to provide it." Michael raised his eyes and cast a steely stare around the room. "This mortal has repented all his former sins and has received Heaven's full and unequivocal absolution. Hell no longer has a claim on either his life or his soul—they both belong to us now."

"You can't do this! You have no right!" Adramelech was shaking, his hands clenched into fists at his side and his feathers rustling.

Michael raised his sword, pointing the tip at Adramelech's chest. "I have *every* right. Step aside, filthy demon, or I will call down the heavenly host, and we will fight to protect our own."

Adramelech glowered, but he made no advance and offered no further resistance. After a drawn-out pause, he spat on the ground near Saul and turned on his heel, storming out of the room. With their leader gone, the other demons made their own swift exits, keeping well clear of Michael and his blade. Less than a minute later, the room was empty, save for the two angels and their charges.

"Thank you, Michael." Baruchiel stepped forward and offered a low bow.

Michael laughed. "I did little, Brother. But the reclaiming of a demon for Heaven is certainly one for the record books." He smiled. "Come, though, it is high time we departed this vile place."

During Baruchiel's exchange with Michael, Tom had rushed to Saul's side and was struggling under his weight as he tried to heft him to his feet. Baruchiel bent down to assist, and between them they got Saul upright and mobile. Baruchiel suddenly remembered his fall, and the way Saul had helped him after. It felt good to be able to return the favour.

With Michael guarding their backs in case any demon should be foolish enough to attack, the group made its way out of the chamber, out of Hell, and back to Earth.

Epilogue

SAUL

Oh, it's you. To be honest, I didn't expect to see you again. I took you for a demon groupie, and there's nothing demonic about me anymore. Well, perhaps 'nothing' is a *slight* exaggeration. I mean, I'm still a devil in the sack, as I'm sure my sweet Tom will attest.

It certainly was a dramatic and unexpected rescue. Took me several days to recover before I started to get my head around it all. Hell, it was a full thirty-six hours before I was even ready to contemplate ravishing Tom— and that's saying something! One thing I can state with absolute certainty is that being de-demonised results in a thumping migraine that would be enough to make anyone repent just about anything. Not that I minded the pain all that much. It's what lets you know you're alive. Isn't that what they say?

Adjusting to mortal life again has been tough at times. If I want my suits to look spick and span nowadays, I have to take them to the dry cleaner. My shirts require ironing by hand. By hand! And I can't handle the heat so well these days, either. If you touch the iron in the wrong spot while it's on, it *really* hurts. Then there's the truly horrifying aging process. Tom declares that I'm being paranoid, seeing things that aren't there, but I fear he's simply trying to spare my feelings. I'm convinced that I have three new grey hairs and at least one new set of crow's feet since my miraculous transformation. I mean, I'm a whole day older today than I was yesterday, and tomorrow I'll be a day older again!

But don't take my minor whingeing as a complaint. By Satan, I'm damn grateful! Finally saying those three little words over which I'd been agonizing for weeks saved me from eternal torment and damnation, and rewarded me with a full lifetime to spend with Tom.

Ah, my sweet Tom. I've never seen him so happy. We're back in London at last, no longer needing to look over our shoulders, free to come and go as we please. Tom's flat was sadly his no longer, but they had stuck all his stuff into storage, so we didn't have to start out on our life together empty-handed. We found a new place to call home in chic, leafy Richmond. Even without my old powers, I was able to sweet-talk the petite, strawberry-blonde saleswoman into offering us a deal we couldn't refuse. Oh yeah, I've still got it, baby!

Tom's drawing comic books again, back in his old job and in his geeky element. His workmates were bemused, to say the least, when he rocked up at the office after five months of radio silence, but he told them he'd been on an impromptu safari in the wilds of Africa—no mobile reception or Internet—and they believed him. I think the photos I found for him online helped. Once we'd edited the images, cutting and pasting the two of us into the scenes, even I'd have been hard-pressed to spot them as fakes.

As for me, a visit to a shady wheeler-dealer I knew from my demon days got me a set of shiny papers that proclaim my new identity—Saul Morgenstern—to the mortal world. (Tom picked out the surname for me. My sweet boy has a wicked, almost devilish, sense of humour these days—my influence, perhaps.) And following my dealings with Miss Strawberry-Blonde at Pickwick, Dorrit & Traddles—I kid you not, that's actually the name of the firm. I couldn't make this stuff up!—I'm contemplating a career in real estate. It seems the perfect job for me: anticipate the client's desires, broker a deal, and then charm them into putting pen to paper. When you think about it, it's not all that different from my former employment, so I should have no trouble fitting in.

I hear the key turn in the lock, and a few seconds later, Tom wraps his arms around me. I sink against him and allow him a moment of supremacy before I twist in his embrace and take back control, claiming his mouth in a deep, breath-defying kiss. When I pull back, there's a gleam in his eye, and I feel a stirring in the depths of my newly reclaimed soul. Okay, I confess, the stirring is as much in a certain part of my anatomy as it is in my soul, but I'm sure the angels won't mind.

I bend down and nibble at Tom's ear, sucking the lobe into my mouth before whispering, "I love you, my sweet Tom."

Tom's reply is an uncharacteristically cocky, "I know."

It's a response more worthy of me than the sweet demi-angel at my side, and one I'm sure he hopes is going to get him fucked, hard and fast, all evening and well into the night. Well, you know me; I'm not so cruel as to dash the boy's hopes now, am I? In fact, it occurs to me that we've not yet gotten around to our previously posited role reversal. Hmm. *Mmm.* I reach down—He's already hard. That's my boy!—and rub him roughly through his jeans. He moans, and the sound sends a spark of pure, undiluted lust straight to my cock, which twitches all the more forcibly as I imagine lowering myself onto Tom's more-than-ample, rigid staff. Naturally, that godawful T-shirt will have to come off first. You know what? It should come off right now! And on that note, I do believe it's high time we moved this *scène d'amour* into the bedroom, *n'est-ce pas?*

So, I guess you and I have reached the end of the road. It's been a wild ride, but it looks like the boy and I are all set to settle down into a life of domestic mortal bliss, and that won't be all that exciting for a voracious voyeur like you. I suppose if you want to swing by to watch the occasional bout of mind-blowing sex, that would be all right. However, if you're looking for something more extreme to get your blood pumping and your neurons firing, you'd better find a new demon to trail. I've exchanged soul scamming for soul sharing and my days of fire and brimstone—the literal kind, anyway—are well and truly behind me.

Now, if you'll excuse me, my sweet boy is waiting, and I'd hate to disappoint him. He and I have important things to do. It's time for us to bring each other a little slice of heaven on earth.

About the Author

Asta Idonea (aka Nicki J Markus) was born in England but now lives in Adelaide, South Australia. She has loved both reading and writing from a young age and is also a keen linguist, having studied several foreign languages.

Asta launched her writing career in 2011 and divides her efforts not only between MM and mainstream works but also between traditional and indie publishing. Her works span the genres, from paranormal to historical and from contemporary to fantasy. It just depends what story and which characters spring into her mind!

As a day job, Asta works as a freelance editor and proofreader, and in her spare time she enjoys music, theater, cinema, photography, and sketching. She also loves history, folklore and mythology, pen-palling, and travel, all of which have provided plenty of inspiration for her writing. She is never found too far from her much-loved library/music room.

Facebook: www.facebook.com/NickiJMarkus

Twitter: @NickiJMarkus

Other books by this author

Old Acquaintance

Of Printers and Presents

Also Available from NineStar Press

Connect with NineStar Press

www.ninestarpress.com

www.facebook.com/ninestarpress

www.facebook.com/groups/NineStarNiche

www.twitter.com/ninestarpress

www.tumblr.com/blog/ninestarpress